**E.D.V**

# Saint of splinters

## A borderline gospel

*For the ones who saw me. My mum, my children, my wife, my family scattered across the world— You each lit a candle in the dark before I knew how to hold a match.*

*And for every soul who ever masked their truth just to be safe—*

*This book is your mirror. You're not alone anymore.*

*Born From Silence, Named in Echo*

"Some fires burn to destroy.
Others burn to light the way.
I was both."

# Contents

# Foreword

**Author's Note — E.D.V.**

This book was never meant to romanticize pain. It wasn't written to dramatize borderline personality disorder or turn chaos into poetry for entertainment's sake.

It was written because I needed you to *see* it.

To understand that BPD isn't just mood swings or messy relationships or the girl who "feels too much." It's a constant war between needing to be loved and being terrified of it. It's writing your own gospel just to feel like something divine might live inside the brokenness. It's loving so hard you bleed for it, then pushing that love away because the fear is louder than the hope.

I wrote this through the lens of how it *feels*. Not how it's diagnosed. Not how it's explained in brochures or DSM checklists. But how it *lives* in the body. How it distorts light. How it turns a kind word into an echo chamber, and silence into abandonment.

Kaela's not a hero. She's not a warning either.

She's a mirror.

For the ones who've ever looked in the mirror and thought: *If I disappear, will anyone notice the shape I left behind?*

I hope you see her.

I hope you see *yourself*—or someone you love—in her pages.

And I hope, more than anything, that it helps you understand that even in the mess, there's meaning. That even cracked things reflect light.

Thank you for walking through the fire with her.

And with me.

This story doesn't follow the rules. Because Kaela doesn't.

Throughout the book, you'll see bracketed text—

*[like this]*

Those aren't typos.

They're interruptions.

Kaela's voice. Raw. Immediate. Unfiltered.

She's not a passive narrator. She's not a prop for your pity or a poster girl for trauma.

She's alive in these pages, ripping the narrative out of the author's hands whenever it starts to get too clean, too poetic, too polished.

She breaks the fourth wall because she was never given one to begin with.

If you hear her sneer, scream, spiral, or seduce you mid-paragraph— good. That's the point.

This isn't just her story.

It's her fight to own it.

So when you see those brackets?

Don't skip them.

That's where the truth lives.

— E.D.V.

# Preface

*Never mind what the kind-sounding author just said.*

**This story is mine.**

**My voice. My way.**

You think you're ready for this?

You're not.

This isn't a book. It's a diagnosis in disguise. It's a mirror you didn't ask for—and once you pick it up, you won't be able to look away.

You want to understand Borderline Personality Disorder?

You want to peek inside the mind of someone who loves like a burning church and breaks like a porcelain scream?

**Good.** Because I'm done explaining myself.

No more DSM footnotes.

No more polite trauma.

This is how it feels.

It feels like craving someone so hard your skin itches with their absence.

Like idealizing a stranger after two eye contacts and a shared joke.

Like sobbing on the bathroom floor because they didn't text back fast enough.

Like being two drinks away from God or a breakdown—and never knowing which altar you're kneeling at.

It's here because I couldn't hold it in anymore.

Because I've choked on silence for too long.

Because being *"too much"* in a world that begs for emotional minimalism will fucking rot you from the inside out.

I don't need you to like me.

I don't need you to save me.

I need you to **see** me—*all of me*—without flinching.

That means the rage. The need. The sex. The spirals.

The way I can want you like oxygen and still ghost you out of fear you'll leave first.

It means the part where I love so loud it makes people run.

This isn't tidy. There's no "arc."

This is BPD, baby.

Sometimes I'm the broken thing.

Sometimes I'm the match.

**So here's the deal:**

You turn this page, and you turn off your judgment.

You don't pity me.

You don't pathologize me.

You don't shrink me to a paragraph in your mental health textbook.

You meet me *here*—where it hurts, where it's holy, where it's **mine**.

And if you're the kind of person who's ever whispered *"I'm too much"* into a pillow?

Welcome home.

Now shut up. I'm talking.

*[lights the match]*

This is how we survive—

By bleeding art from agony.

By screaming love into the void and calling it poetry.

By getting high on validation and crashing in silence.

You want calm?

You want tidy recovery arcs and inspirational quotes?
**Fuck off.**
This is a gospel written in blood.
A story that doesn't tie itself up with a bow—
Because some of us are made of **splinters** and **fire**.
And that's still beautiful.
So if you're brave—if you're broken enough to be honest—
Turn the page.
Feel what we feel.
Love like it'll kill you.
Grieve like you'll never stop.
Dissociate. Spiral.
Hope anyway.
And above all, remember this:

> *We are not too much.*
> *The world is just too numb.*

It's BPD with lipstick smeared, fingers trembling, mascara running like rivers of rage.
It's the truth.
The ugly, sacred, desperate truth.
It's the scream beneath the smile.
The red beneath the gloss.
Kaela isn't your hero.
She's not your cautionary tale either.
She's just the girl who felt everything—
And dared to speak it.
And if that scares you?
**Good.**
Because healing isn't always pretty.

Sometimes it looks like fire.

Sometimes it *is*.

**Turn the page.**

**Light the match.**

**Let the splinters speak.**

And if you're not crying yet?

…You will be.

*I promise.*

[OH AND IF THE AUTHOR'S DOING THAT WHOLESOME "I JUST WANT TO TELL A STORY" THING.

ADORABLE.

SHAME THIS STORY IS MINE.

SO IF YOU SEE BRACKETS, BABY—

THAT'S ME CLEANING UP HIS MESS.

ENJOY.]

# Acknowledgments

To every soul who ever felt too loud, too raw, too much for this numbed-out world—this is for you.

To my clients—my chosen family on the edges—you've taught me more about survival, grace, and honesty than any therapist's notes ever could. You showed me what healing looks like when no one else believed it was possible.

To the people who called me unstable, overdramatic, or unfit—thank you. You handed me the match. I lit the page.

To my wife—you are my grounding wire and my flame. You held space for me when I was all static, and stood your ground when I couldn't find mine. Because of you, I built a home, a legacy, and the strength to write what once felt unspeakable.

To my son—you are proof that love can be gentle and fierce at the same time. Your light refracts through every word in this book. If Kaela is a prism, you were the first spectrum I ever truly saw.

To my daughters—one oceans away, one right here beside me. You are my bravery in motion. To my daughter in the UK: your strength echoes across distance, and I feel your brilliance every single day. To my stepdaughter here at home: your resilience is unmatched, and your quiet power humbles me.

To my niece—thank you for holding the earliest drafts of my truth without flinching. Your support lit a path through the fear.

To my mum—you gave me permission to be myself before I even knew who that was. You loved me across continents and contradictions. Because of you, I know what unconditional means.

To my brother in Canada and my sister in Scotland—you are living proof that distance doesn't dissolve connection. Your threads are still woven into this tapestry.

To my dad—

Thank you for the roof, the labor, the quiet sacrifices I didn't see until I grew up. You gave us everything you had, and I carry it with me now—proudly.

To the neurodivergent community—you helped me name the fire that lived in my chest. You gave me the language I spent a lifetime mimicking without words. This book is for us—the ones who feel everything and survive anyway.

To those who see themselves in Kaela—your story isn't shameful. It's sacred.

And to you, reader—if you made it this far, if something in Kaela's chaos mirrored your own, if her truths landed like echoes in your ribcage—

Then maybe, just maybe, you're not alone after all.

We are not too much.

We are the splinters.
   We are the fire.
   We are still burning.

With defiance, tenderness, and deep gratitude,
   —E.D.V.

**One**

# "The Temperature Here Is Too Loud"

She stepped off the plane and into hell's armpit.

Gold Coast heat didn't greet her—it assaulted her like a fever dream in drag. Hot, wet, hostile. The air tasted like melted sugar, sunscreen sex, and the ghost of a forest fire.

Her Danish body clenched in revolt. She'd grown up on grey skies and the hum of buses through snow. Rain that knew its place. Cold that left you alone. Not this. Not this *loudness* of air.

She blinked against the sun. Sweat bloomed instantly under her arms. Her mask—smooth, pleasant, professionally Danish—stayed locked in place.

Customs was a blur. A smiling man asked, "Business or pleasure?" and her brain took one full second too long to answer.

"Working holiday," she said, voice clean, accent shaved. Perfect little immigrant. Ready to contribute.

He nodded and waved her through.

As she walked, she caught her reflection in a brushed metal panel: pale, flushed, already shining with sweat. A girl stretched too thin

1

between a past and a lie.

*New country. New name. New performance.*

Baggage claim was a war zone. Children screamed in stereo. A man in a straw hat offered his Instagram handle to a woman who looked like she'd rather eat glass. Everything smelled like mango and melting plastic.

Kaela moved like a ghost. Every movement calculated. Measured. Invisible.

She retrieved her suitcase—cheap, floral, secondhand—and dodged a group of men loudly chanting something about tequila. One of them stumbled and spilled beer on his flip-flop.

*Tosse,* she thought, too tired to scowl. Idiot, sure—but Danish idiocy was mild. This? This was a *dangerous* kind of dumb. The kind that'd call you babe while pissing on your suitcase.

Her phone buzzed.

**ROOM 3B**
**CODE: 1197**
**WIFI: NO PASSWORD**
**ENJOY YOUR STAY :)**

*Hyggeligt,* she thought, yeah right!

Nothing about this was hyggeligt. No warmth, no candles, no slow conversation over coffee. Just neon optimism and forced intimacy with strangers who'd overshare by breakfast.

The hostel receptionist had a lanyard of keycards and the personality of a golden retriever. Kaela gave her best smile. Practised. Closed-lip. Nondescript. Scandinavian Pleasant™.

Room 3B was a box with a ceiling fan older than she was.

She dropped her suitcase and peeled her clothes off like guilt. Her body was a betrayal—sweat-soaked, dizzy, aching behind the eyes.

She stepped into the shower and turned it full cold.

She lasted maybe two minutes before her knees gave out.

Tiles. Her cheek pressed against cold ceramic. The heat above from the *fucking heat lamps*—like someone installed Satan as the electrician.

And then the nausea hit. Hard. She vomited down the drain, sobbing quietly into the floor.

The water kept running.

*[OH YEAH. GLAMOROUS IMMIGRANT LIFE, BABY.*
*STEP ONE: VOMIT IN A FOREIGN SHOWER.*
*STEP TWO: PRETEND YOU'RE STRONG.*
*STEP THREE: CHOKE ON YOUR OWN EXPECTATIONS.]*

*Hvorfor helvede er der varmelamper i et land som det her?*

Why the hell were there heat lamps in a country like this?

She curled onto her side, body shaking, water hitting her back like mockery. This wasn't weather. This was punishment.

*Jeg kan ikke gøre det her.*

I can't do this.

She thought of Amagerbrogade. The tram tracks. The little bakery with the cardamom buns. Cold mornings where people left you alone. Where *ro* wasn't something you begged for—it was built into the silence between strangers.

Here? Here the silence was always one drunk tourist away from being shattered.

She stayed there until the water ran lukewarm.

She stepped outside and the city slapped her again.

The Gold Coast was a migraine dressed in sequins. Every surface gleamed. Every smell fought for dominance. Coconut, weed, fried chicken, wet cement. The air was alive with tourists yelling, gulls screeching, and that specific kind of laugh you only hear in places where people pay to forget who they are.

The sun was still hunting her. Her body couldn't decide whether to sweat or shut down.

Her backpack stuck to her spine like a second skin.

*Hvor er skyggen?* she thought. Where the fuck is the shade?

A tram rolled past, plastered in ads for surfing lessons and sex shows. She caught her reflection in the window again—face blotchy, mascara tired, mouth slightly open like she'd forgotten how to close it.

She looked like someone halfway between overdosing on life and quietly combusting from the inside out.

Her hostel sat just off the main strip, tucked between a tattoo parlour and a Korean BBQ place that smelled like scorched heaven. The windows had bars. The door buzzed when she pushed it. Inside, it was only slightly cooler, and somehow *wetter*. The walls sweated with her.

The elevator now didn't work. Of course it didn't. She dragged her ass up three flights of stairs, her legs threatening a strike.

Room 3B was smaller in the daylight. The fan did fuck-all just pushed around hot air. The curtains were floral and tragic.

She lay on the bed and stared at the ceiling, letting her body pulse like a dying star.

She imagined sending a text to someone back home.

*Hej, det er for varmt her. Jeg kan ikke trække vejret. Jeg tror, jeg dør.*

Hi, it's too hot here. I can't breathe. I think I'm dying.

But there was no one to send it to.

Later, she found a 7-Eleven and bought an iced coffee that tasted like despair and sugar. Sat on a bench under a plastic palm tree and watched people live loudly.

Everyone here looked like they'd been *designed*. Blonde, tanned, sculpted. Even the kids had abs. Kaela felt like a walking oil slick.

She watched a couple kiss too loudly. A girl film herself sipping

4

bubble tea like it was her last act on earth. A busker in a bucket hat sang "Wonderwall" like it was gospel.

She stared straight ahead and thought:

*You don't belong here.*

*You don't belong anywhere.*

*You are too pale, too soft, too full of static to be this loud.*

She drank the coffee anyway.

The bar was called **Dusk**, and nothing about it matched the name.

Inside, it was fluorescent as hell. Pale purple lighting over fake leather booths. A jukebox that played pop hits from five years ago. Mirrors behind the bar smudged with fingerprints and regret. The air stank of sugar, disinfectant, and lime cordial that had never seen a lime.

Kaela stepped in and felt her soul retract.

She was overdressed. Underdone. Her hair was tied too tight and her skin still glistened from the walk over. She wiped her palms on her thighs and tried to remember how to act like someone worth hiring.

The manager sat at a high-top near the door, chewing gum like it owed her rent. Her nametag said **Dani**, and her nails were chipped in a way that looked intentional.

"You Kaela?" she asked, already bored.

Kaela nodded. "Yes. Hi."

"You got RSA?"

"Yes."

(She'd passed it online while half-asleep in a Danish winter, sipping lukewarm tea and wondering what the fuck a "standard drinks chart" even was.)

"You ever bartended before?"

"A little."

"You hot?"

Kaela blinked.

Dani rolled her eyes. "As in—can you handle the heat, babe? We get packed. Gets sweaty."

"Oh. Yes. Sure."

Lie. The sweat behind her knees was planning a rebellion.

Dani gave her a once-over that felt like an X-ray. "You'll do. Trial shift Friday. Black pants, no heels, hair up. Don't steal from the till and don't fuck the customers unless they're hot."

Kaela opened her mouth to respond but got interrupted by movement behind the bar.

And then she saw him.

Iver.

T-shirt. Jeans. Golden tan. Soft arms with light freckles. A smile like sun filtering through curtains. The kind of smile that made you forget to breathe for a second.

He was wiping down the bar, but looked up when Dani said, "Iver—this is the new one."

His eyes met Kaela's.

And for a second—just one fuck-you-to-reality second—she felt *seen*.

Not like stared-at. Not like assessed or filtered or tagged.

*Seen.*

She hated it immediately.

"Hey," he said, voice warm. "Welcome to hell."

Kaela let out a breath she hadn't realised she was holding. Smiled, just barely.

"Thanks," she said. "It's hotter than I expected."

Iver grinned. "You get used to it. Eventually."

She doubted that. She was still sweating in places she hadn't known could sweat.

Dani waved a hand. "Trial on Friday. If she dies, we'll replace her."

Iver shrugged. "Fair enough."

Kaela nodded, muttered a thank you, and walked out into the blinding sun like she'd just survived a baptism in bleach.

She didn't walk home. She drifted.

Down past souvenir shops, sex shops, and sushi joints. Her body buzzed with residual adrenaline and salt. The sweat had dried in itchy constellations across her ribs. Her mouth still tasted like artificial lime and social panic.

Iver's smile haunted her like a song she didn't know the lyrics to. Something warm. Something dangerous. Something that threatened to unmask her without even trying.

She lit a cigarette outside the hostel even though she didn't smoke. Not really. But her hands needed something to do and her mouth needed an excuse to stay closed.

It burned fast in the wind. She let it.

*Why did he look at me like that?*

Not in a predatory way. Not even flirty. Just—open. Like she was something new and he hadn't decided how to feel about her yet. Like he'd seen all the cracks and didn't flinch.

It made her stomach twist. Made her spine itch.

Kindness was always a trick. In her experience, smiles were the loading screens before the crash.

The bathroom mirror had fogged by the time she got upstairs. She hadn't even turned on the shower yet—just stood there, watching the heat lamps hum like a threat.

*Who the fuck needs heat in this kind of weather?*

Australians, apparently. All sunburn and smiles and overconfidence.

She stripped down again and stepped under the cold. Her body was trembling, jaw clenched, skin humming with leftover salt and adrenaline. She leaned into the tiles and let the water hit her like a baptism she didn't ask for.

This place wasn't welcoming. It was *hostile with a smile.*

And Iver's voice played again:

*"Welcome to hell."*

7

He meant the bar. But it fit the whole fucking country.

When she returned to the room, she didn't bother with a towel. She was too hot. Too raw. Too exhausted to give a fuck.

Kaela collapsed naked onto the bed, water still dripping from her thighs, the fan spinning overhead like a lazy god. The sheets were pushed aside. Fuck covers. Fuck shame. She sprawled out like a melting starfish and let the air dry her skin in patches.

The room was shared. Probably mixed.

She didn't care.

**[OH LOOK, NAKED GIRL ON A BED—FEEL SOMETHING YET? THIS ISN'T SEXUAL. THIS IS SURVIVAL.**

**IF YOU'RE WAITING FOR THE CAMERA TO PAN DOWN, CONGRATS, YOU'RE PART OF THE PROBLEM.]**

Danes didn't do shame when it came to the body. Nudity wasn't scandalous. It was *normal*. Sensible. Efficient. If someone stared, that was their problem, not hers.

She exhaled.

Sweat clung to her in spite of the cold shower. Her hair stuck to the pillow. Every part of her pulsed with heat and residual panic.

Her phone buzzed. Hostel group chat: memes, party invites, someone asking if anyone had a spare towel.

She turned it face-down.

And whispered to the ceiling:

*"I don't want to be seen."*

But the part she didn't say—the truth baked into her bones—was:

*I do.*

*I just want it to feel safe when it happens.*

**[OKAY, BUT—NAKED ON A BED IN A MIXED HOSTEL ROOM?**

*THAT'S NOT "DON'T LOOK AT ME" ENERGY.*
*THAT'S "LOOK AT ME, BUT ONLY IF YOU SEE ME RIGHT."*
*WHICH IS THE SAME AS SAYING: NEVER.]*

# Two

## *"Smiles with Teeth"*

She woke with her mouth dry and her skin wetter than it had any right to be. The fan overhead buzzed like a lazy wasp, pushing hot air in reluctant spirals. Her thighs stuck together. Her hair had dried into a crown of static.

One bunk over, a man snored softly.

Kaela stared at the ceiling.

She *knew* it was a mixed dorm. Had known when she booked it. Knew it when she checked in. Knew it last night when she fell asleep naked on top of the sheets with her dignity melting into the mattress.

But *knowing* something doesn't mean your body agrees.

*[YOU EVER TRY EXPLAINING THAT TO A THERAPIST? THAT YOUR BODY FEELS UNSAFE EVEN WHEN NOTHING "HAPPENED"? YEAH, ME NEITHER.]*

She turned her head, just slightly. He was young. Twenty-something. Shoes off. Shirt off. Blanket half-kicked away. He was sprawled like a man who'd never had to shrink himself to stay safe. Breathing evenly. Vulnerable in that loud, male way.

He hadn't touched her. Hadn't even looked at her, as far as she could tell.

And still, her stomach clenched.

Not with fear—more like *readiness*. The kind of readiness you learn young when the world teaches you to make yourself small just in case.

Danes didn't flinch at nudity. Co-ed spaces were normal. Bodies weren't threats unless someone made them so.

But Kaela wasn't in Denmark anymore.

Here, even sleeping felt political.

She rose quietly, padding to the bathroom in silence. No eye contact. No words. Her footsteps soft, her breath softer. The floor cool under her toes. The mirror showed a girl still half-drowned in salt and sleep. Mascara ghosting under her eyes. Neck blotchy. Expression unreadable.

She rinsed her face with cold water and whispered, "Du er okay," to the girl in the mirror.

You're okay.

She didn't feel it. But she said it anyway.

The bathroom light flickered above her.

Outside, the Gold Coast screamed in colour.

Kaela learned quickly.

Not the job—that was easy. Tap the keg, wipe the bar, upsell the cocktails with names like "Wet Ass Wallaby" and "Tropical Slut." Smile. Nod. Laugh on cue like an actor in a sitcom no one's watching.

No—the real lesson was cultural. **Aussie Nice.**

The religion of the surface.

Everyone smiled here. Big, toothy, relentless grins. You'd think the whole country was on MDMA and sunstroke.

Coworkers called her "gorgeous" and "love" and "babe" like they were flipping through a script. They'd slap her back, tell her she was doing "great, mate" even when she spilled a tray of glasses and said *fuck* under her breath loud enough to echo.

She adapted. That was what she did.

Mask tighter. Movements smoother. Voice bright.

Inside, she itched.

The bar had no shade. Just mirrors and purple neon, like working inside a nightclub-themed microwave. Sweat lived under her bra strap now. Her uniform clung like consequence.

Dani, the manager, had two modes: bored or biting. Today it was biting.

"Oi, Copenhagen, you alive in there?"

Kaela blinked. "Yeah. Sorry."

"You've been wiping the same bit of counter for five minutes."

Had she?

She looked down. Yeah. Foam gone. Just swirling water and distraction.

"Long shift," she said.

Dani shrugged. "Welcome to hospitality, sweetheart."

She walked away before Kaela could think of a retort. Not that she would've said one. That wasn't how you survived here.

Iver leaned over during clean-up. Close enough to smell the citrus of his cologne. He reached around her for a glass and let his arm brush hers. Not creepy. Just casual.

Too casual.

"Always this focused?" he asked, smirking.

She looked up. Smile already locked. "Sorry?"

"You clean like you're angry at the bacteria."

She laughed, soft and hollow. "I like a spotless bar."

He didn't back away. Just watched her for a beat longer than necessary. His freckles looked like a galaxy scattered across sunburned

12

skin.

"You're different," he said finally.

Her stomach flipped.

She knew what he meant. But what she *heard* was:

**You're mine.**

It was always like that. Compliments came with subtext. She'd spent years trying to decode the undertones of praise. Sometimes it was admiration. Sometimes it was ownership.

She didn't know which scared her more.

Iver moved on, humming to himself as he stacked glasses. Kaela stood still, staring at the countertop, her rag dripping onto her shoes.

She smiled. Of course she smiled.

Because that's what you do when someone nice makes you nervous in a country that worships chill.

They all went out after the shift.

No one really *asked*—they just moved like a tide, and Kaela let herself be pulled under. That's what passing meant: *go where they go, laugh when they laugh, drink when they drink.*

The air was thick with heat and half-price margaritas. They sat outside a bar called *Sin Bin*, surrounded by LED-lit menus and plastic plants that sweated in the dark. The music was too loud to talk properly, which Kaela appreciated. Less room to get it wrong.

Iver bought her a drink.

Something pink with a wedge of watermelon and a name she didn't catch.

It tasted like fruit syrup, chemical pink—and melted anxiety.

"You've got this calm thing going on," he said, tipping his head like he was studying her. "Like... you've seen some shit but you're still standing."

She smiled. Tight. Measured. "I'm Danish."

He laughed. "Is that code?"

13

"Maybe."

He didn't press. Just nodded and took a sip of his beer. His gaze wandered back to the group, leaving Kaela with her pulse and her paranoia.

She stared out toward the sea. Even from this far inland, the Gold Coast glimmered with that beachy promise. Palm trees under spotlights. A moon too smug. Waves that whispered like gossip.

There was a jellyfish on the sand. Pink. Translucent. It pulsed in slow agony as a seagull pecked at it.

She took out her phone and snapped a photo without thinking.

"Even the sea stings here."

She wrote it in her notes app. No context. No punctuation. Just the truth, bleeding through in lowercase.

Later, in bed, she couldn't sleep.

The ceiling fan creaked like an old man's knees. The air stuck to her chest like regret.

She opened her journal and started to write.

Not full sentences. Just *fragments*.

My hands feel too loud. My mouth won't shut up, even when it's closed
  the sun is a fucking liar
  he looked at me like i might unravel in his hands
  why does kindness feel like a dare
  i can't find my voice in this country
  everything tastes like teeth

**[AND I'M THE ONE WITH THE "PERSONALITY DISOR-DER"? SURE, JAN.]**

14

She stared at the page. The ink shimmered slightly where her sweat hit the corner.

Then she closed the book.

Smiled to herself.

And whispered: "What the fuck is happening to me?"

Morning came like a slap.

Sunlight pierced through the floral curtains, already hot. Her mouth tasted like artificial watermelon and sleep paralysis. She rolled onto her back, groaned, then sat up too fast. The room spun briefly, threatening rebellion.

The guy from the other bed was gone. No snoring. No signs of life except a towel hanging over the bunk rail and a tangle of headphones on the floor.

She exhaled.

Not relief. Just space.

Her journal lay open on the nightstand. She didn't remember leaving it that way. Didn't remember much, actually—just the fragments, written in script that looked more like someone else's voice than her own.

She read a line again.

"Why does kindness feel like a dare?"

**[BECAUSE IT FUCKING IS.]**

It hit harder in daylight.

Work was fine. She was fine. Everyone was *fine*.

Kaela said all the right things at all the right volumes. She laughed at jokes she barely heard. She passed drinks. Wiped counters. Smiled with teeth.

Every time Iver walked past, her skin buzzed like feedback.

15

Not bad. Not good. Just—*too much.* Like standing too close to a speaker during someone else's favourite song.

She caught her reflection in the bar's back mirror. Mascara precise. Lips tinted a little too pink. Smile rehearsed. Hands still.

She looked perfect.

She hated it.

That night, someone on the hostel balcony told a story about hooking up with a scuba instructor in Bali. Everyone laughed. Kaela laughed too. Louder than she meant to. Sharper.

Like she was trying to saw through something.

A guy offered her a drink and she declined. Politely. He shrugged and turned to someone blonder. Her stomach unclenched.

—

She stepped into the shared bathroom and found it fogged with mirror mist. Someone had drawn a heart in the condensation. Kaela wiped it away.

Behind her, the light flickered.

She stared at herself.

Lifted her mouth into that smile—the one that said I'm fine, I'm normal, I'm easy to love.

Held it.

Watched it twitch.

*"Who the fuck are you smiling for?"* she whispered.

**[SPOILER: IT'S NEVER FOR ME.]**

## Three

# Journal Entry 1

I can't tell if I'm invisible or just unbearable.

People smile at me like I'm a screensaver. Pretty. Harmless. Empty.

And I smile back like I'm not screaming under my skin.

Today I said "I'm fine" seven times. I counted.
   Every single time meant something different.
   Every single time was a lie.

I keep thinking if I make myself quiet enough, small enough, smooth enough—
   someone will love me by accident.
   Like it'll just slip out of them before they can stop it.

I want someone to say I see you and mean it.
   Not the curated version.

Not the nice-girl-mask with polite pain and digestible darkness.
I want to be seen like roadkill.
Like something you can't look at without feeling changed.

But I don't want to ask for it.
Because then they'll say I'm needy. Clingy. A mess.

I hate being a mess.
I hate pretending I'm not.

Sometimes I look in the mirror and wonder—
Would I even like me if I didn't know what it felt like to be me?

I'm scared of what the answer might be.

*[WAIT.*
*WHAT THE ACTUAL FUCK IS THIS DOING HERE?*
*IS THIS A JOKE?*
*YOU—YOU PUBLISHED THIS?!*

*Why not go all the way?*
*Why not pin me to a wall and let them sniff my fucking thoughts?*

*Jesus.*
*This wasn't for them.*
*This was mine.*
*The one place I could be disgusting and divine and dangerous and*
*safe all at once.*

*But no.*
  *You couldn't resist, could you?*

*You actually turned my breakdown into a bedtime story.*
  *Wrapped it in metaphor and handed it out like candy at a trauma carnival.*

*This was mine.*
  *My ink.*
  *My silence.*
  *My blood on the goddamn page.*

*And you served it up like it's just another quirky character note in your little trauma novel.]*

# Four

## *"You're Not Supposed to Feel That Much"*

Her phone screen glowed like judgment.

She'd waited twenty-three minutes and seventeen seconds before texting him back. That was the polite window, right? Not too eager. Not too cold. Just casually interested. Just the right amount of chill to seem effortless.

Except it wasn't fucking effortless. Her thumb had hovered over the send button like it was wired to explosives.

**kaela:**
*last night was fun. hope i didn't come off too weird, lol*
And his reply?

   *iver:*
   *all good*

That smiley face was violence.

Not the good kind. Not the *you're cute* kind. The kind that felt like being patted on the head and dismissed. Pitying. Distance with a smile glued on.

She stared at it for a full five minutes. Her chest got tight. Her jaw clenched. The world went too bright around the edges.

Her brain spiralled. Loud. Ruthless. Unforgiving.

He's bored of you already.

You came on too strong.

You're not mysterious, you're unstable.

Why would someone like him want someone like you?

Kaela reread her own message.

Again. And again.

Her fingers curled around the edge of the bed.

Jordan was at the desk across the room, headphones in, laptop open. She knew his name—*Jordan*—from a short, neutral introduction when he moved in last week. He'd said it with zero flair, zero expectation. Just a fact. She hadn't offered hers.

Probably editing video or building something with code. The screen reflected in his glasses—orange-blue flickers of a world more structured than hers.

He hadn't said a word. He never did when she was in this state.

But she caught him glance up, once.

Just once.

She dropped the phone face-down on the pillow and smiled at the ceiling. A smile with no roots. No warmth.

A smile with teeth.

The door clicked shut behind her, and the bathroom swallowed her whole.

She slid the lock. Sat on the toilet lid. Exhaled.

Then she folded in on herself like bad news.

Her chest was a scream.

Not out loud—not ever.

But inside, it roared like a siren wrapped in gauze.

**[OH, PLEASE—DON'T TELL ME YOU'RE GONNA DESCRIBE THIS LIKE IT'S POETIC. IT'S SNOT AND SILENCE AND I'M SICK OF YOUR PRETTY FUCKING SENTENCES.]**

*He doesn't like you. He doesn't want you. You were stupid to text him. You should've said nothing. You always ruin it.*

The spiral had teeth tonight. Gnawed its way down her spine.

Kaela hugged her knees and pressed her face into the crook of her elbow. Her breath hitched. The ache behind her eyes bloomed hot, sharp, too close to real.

She bit her lip. Hard. She wouldn't cry.

She wouldn't—

Her nails dug into the meat of her thighs, hard enough to leave little crescents of proof. She needed *something* solid. Something louder than her brain. Pain was clean. Understandable.

One breath. Two.

And then it broke.

A sob clawed its way out, ugly and wet, and she tried to swallow it down. The tiles were cold against her feet. Her whole body shook like a blown speaker.

She didn't scream.

She never screamed.

She *leaked.*

Quiet. Private. An implosion behind closed doors. Just enough to feel the burn, not enough to make a sound anyone else could hear.

Her phone buzzed once in her pocket.

She didn't look.

She stayed like that for ten minutes. Maybe twenty. Time didn't live here.

Eventually, she stood. Rinsed her face. Stared into the mirror until her expression stopped twitching.

Then she smiled.

Mascara streaks and all.

The mask slipped back on like muscle memory.

Kaela was up before her alarm.

It wasn't rest. It was resignation.

She moved like someone pretending to have slept. Like a ghost play-acting human. Showered. Dressed. Foundation just thick enough to cover the blotches under her eyes. Concealer like war paint.

Her hair went up into a ponytail so tight it gave her a tension headache by default. Clean shirt. Black pants. Neutral lips. Smile in the mirror—rehearsed, solid, unremarkable.

*Be invisible in the right ways. Presentable. Not penetrable.*

## [WELCOME TO THE NEUROTIC OLYMPICS—WHERE I WIN GOLD IN EMOTIONAL CAMOUFLAGE.]

She stepped out into the hallway just as Jordan was heading to the showers, towel over one shoulder, tablet in hand like he'd forgotten to put it down mid-thought.

He didn't flinch when they passed each other.

"Morning," he said casually, not even looking up from his screen.

Kaela nodded, already halfway down the stairs.

The tram was late. The platform was humid. She stood in a sea of tank tops and work uniforms, pretending not to exist.

Work was fluorescent and fast.

The blender screamed. The ice bucket overflowed. People laughed about shit she didn't understand. Everything was louder than her thoughts, which was almost comforting.

She smiled. She joked. She remembered how many limes Dani liked in her gin and how to shake a mojito without spilling.

Nobody noticed.

And if they did, they didn't care.

That was the beauty of places like this—you could be unraveling in real time and still nail the lunch rush.

*Smile like it's armor.*

*Smile like you mean it.*

*Smile until it becomes real.*

She even laughed at something Iver said. Loud enough to sound natural. Quiet enough not to cling.

He wasn't cold.

He just wasn't... anything.

And that was worse.

She was restocking the lemon wedges when it happened.

Iver walked in with his usual unbothered breeze—hood up, sunnies on, like the sun was his personal spotlight. She didn't expect much. A nod, maybe. A grunt. A casual *hey*.

Instead, he grinned like a warm drink in winter and stepped behind the bar.

"Didn't think you'd survive last night's chaos," he said, voice low, amused.

Then—just like that—he leaned in and kissed her on the cheek.

Not flirtatious.

Not romantic.

Just a gesture. Small. Offhand. Uncomplicated.

But Kaela's body betrayed her.

Her spine straightened. Her lungs released a breath she didn't realise she'd been strangling. Her stomach flipped like a dropped glass, and heat bloomed in her face like shame.

She smiled. Reflex. Too wide. Too bright.

He was already reaching for a rag to wipe down the bar.

No lingering gaze. No follow-up flirt. Just normal Iver.

Like nothing had been wrong.

Like she hadn't spent the last twelve hours dying inside and resurrecting herself in the mirror.

She turned back to the lemons.

Her hands were shaking.

You're not supposed to feel this much. It's just a cheek kiss.

It's not a declaration. It's not a promise.

But her chest was singing anyway. Dissonant. Messy. Real.

She wanted to scream. Or cry. Or kiss him back. Or disappear entirely.

Instead, she stacked lemons and swallowed herself whole.

# Five

## Validation Is a Drug

She woke up sticky with him.

Kaela didn't know if it was her room or his. The ceiling fan was spinning too slow, the bedsheets kicked into a nest of breath and bruises. Her thighs ached. Her throat was dry. Her skin smelled like sweat, lube, and last night's perfume clawing for relevance.

Iver was next to her. On his back, arm draped lazily over his eyes, chest rising like nothing mattered.

She stared.

The rise and fall of him. The shape of him. The stupid curve of his mouth like he'd just dreamed about getting away with something.

She felt high.

Not on drugs. Not on love. On him.

On the fucking *fact* that he'd wanted her, touched her, moaned her name against her ribs like it meant something.

Validation soaked into her pores like heat.

His hands had been everywhere—hungry, thoughtless, reverent and rushed. He kissed like he was trying to shut her up, like he didn't trust words but worshipped mouths. She'd melted under him, around him, into him, because it was the closest she'd come to being *real* in days.

He made her feel solid.

He made her forget the storm under her skin.

He made her vanish and return in one breath.

But the comedown...

The comedown was brutal.

Because now he wasn't touching her.

He wasn't looking at her.

He wasn't doing anything *for* her.

And she felt herself start to vanish again.

He was already moving.

Not fast—just casually reclaiming his limbs. Pulling on boxers, then jeans, then that same worn shirt from last night. The one she'd grabbed at like a lifeline, fingers curled in cotton and desperation.

Kaela stayed still.

Pretending to be asleep felt easier than speaking. Easier than facing the moment his eyes would pass over her body like a checklist. Something touched. Something used. Something not broken, just... done.

She opened one eye as he turned to grab his phone off the floor.

His face lit up in the blue glow. He smirked. Tapped something. Probably a meme. Probably some group chat she wasn't part of.

Not a single glance back at her.

Say something, *she thought.*

Touch me again.

Lie and say it meant something.

But his silence wasn't cruel. That was the worst part.

It was kind.

Casual.

Comfortable in that way that meant it hadn't touched him the same way.

He stretched. Yawned. Looked around.

"Shit," he muttered. "Gotta grab a Red Bull before work."

Then finally—finally—his eyes landed on her.

"You awake?"

Kaela nodded, swallowing a desert behind her tongue.

He smiled. That lazy, sun-drunk smile.

"Last night was fun."

"Yeah," she said. "It was."

He kissed her forehead.

Like a goddamn *brother*.

Like a reward for being cool about everything.

Then he was gone.

Door clicking shut like punctuation.

She stared at the ceiling.

Her skin still burned with the memory of him, but now it felt less like worship and more like residue. Like graffiti on a bathroom wall.

*[You're still here, huh? Enjoying the tragedy? Is this fun for you? Watching me come undone in high-def?]*

Her fingers itched. She grabbed her journal—floral cover, half full of curated nothing—and flipped to a blank page.

Then she wrote:

I am only real when someone else is touching me.

I don't exist between texts.

If no one looks at me, I disappear.

She paused.

Then, smaller:

Why doesn't he see it?

Why don't I matter when he's not inside me?

The page blurred.

She didn't cry.

She just turned on her phone and stared at it until the screen dimmed again.

Nothing.

No message.

No "thinking about you."

Just silence.

And her reflection, faint in the glass.

Too much makeup. Too much hope. Too much.

She didn't even like vodka.

But she drank it anyway.

Straight, fast, mechanical. Like she could disinfect the ache. Like she could kill the part of her that gave a shit.

The bar was full of people who were too loud and not loud enough. Everything thumped—music, feet, voices—all of it shaking her spine like a warning. Her laugh came easy tonight. Sharp. Overbright. Glittery with lies.

Iver was there. Of course he was. Laughing with customers, leaning on the bar like he owned gravity. He ruffled her hair once in passing, and she practically lit up like an overworked fuse box.

"Someone's in a good mood," he teased.

She smiled. Bit her lip. Tried to act like it was casual.

"Vodka agrees with me."

"You're chill as," he said. "Love it."

That word—*chill*—hit like a slap in satin.

She wanted to scream. To grab him by the shoulders and say: *Do you not see this fire? Do you not feel how loud I am under my skin?*

But she just laughed again and poured a round of lemon drops for the hens at table six.

They clapped.

She curtsied.

It was all theatre now. Emotional burlesque. Let them tip her in attention.

You're so fun.

You're a vibe.

You're easy to talk to.

None of it meant anything.

Kaela danced behind the bar like her own ghost. Her voice pitched up. Her jokes came faster. She leaned closer to strangers and smiled like her life depended on it.

Because it did.

Because if she didn't hold their attention, she wasn't *real.*

Because if he wasn't looking at her, she wasn't *anything.*

The validation came in flashes—his hand grazing her hip, his glance when she poured a drink right. But they never lingered.

Nothing lingered anymore.

Except the ache.
Except her.

She fucked him like she needed to be rewritten.

Not loved. Not held.
*Erased and redrawn.*
Every kiss was a plea.
Every moan was a confession she didn't want to speak.
She pulled him into her like a storm, wrapped her thighs around him like salvation, dug her nails into his back just to leave a mark. Just to prove she'd been there. That she'd mattered.
He whispered her name against her throat and it almost sounded like worship.
Almost.
After, his breath slowed. His grip loosened. He rolled away to check his phone.
She watched him without blinking.
He was scrolling. Laughing softly. Thumb dancing over glass like it mattered more than her pulse, still skittering under her ribs.

Look at me again, *she thought.*
Make me matter again.

She reached out—just touched his arm.
"Do you like me?" she whispered.
It slipped out.
Not planned. Not polished. Just naked. Just bleeding.
He looked up.
Confused.
Then smiled, soft. Not cruel.

"You're hot," he said. "Obviously."

Obviously.

Her chest cracked, clean and quiet.

She nodded. Said "Thanks," like it was a compliment. Like it answered the question.

He kissed her forehead—again with that fucking gentleness.

Then he rolled over and turned out the light.

She lay there in the dark, eyes wide, ribs echoing.

Not alone.

But lonelier than ever.

*[And here you are again. Watching. Scribbling metaphors like they're balm. You think if you make it beautiful enough, it won't hurt as much?*

*Newsflash: it still fucking hurts!.]*

## Six

# "The Party Where I Drowned and No One Noticed"

It hit her the moment she stepped through the door—

Noise.

Not music. Not rhythm. Just noise.
  Like someone had taken joy and compressed it into a migraine.
  Basslines like punches. Lights like electric knives.

People pulsed in time with the chaos—sweaty, glittering, loud.

Kaela blinked once, and the room doubled. Blinked again, and the floor tilted.

She was already too much. And this?
  This was more.

Her body knew it first—
    the tightness in her chest,
    the way her spine locked in rebellion.
    Every smile around her looked like a barbed wire fence.

She tried to smile back.
    Tried to remember how it went.
    Upturn lips. Chin forward. Head tilt. Show teeth.
    Human.exe running smooth.

Someone shoved a drink into her hand.
    Something purple and glowing and criminally sweet.
    She drank it. Fast. Let it coat her throat like denial.

*[What? You thought this would be a fun scene? Some flirty little glitter romp?*
    *No, sweetheart. This is how the soul evacuates through skin.]*

"Iver's here!" someone shouted, but it felt like an accusation.
    Like she'd shown up late to a story she wasn't invited to.

She spotted him near the kitchen.
    Red solo cup in hand, laughing, radiant.
    His face haloed by the fridge light and bad decisions.

He shouted her name—across the crowd, across the static.
    "Kaela!"

It cracked through the mess like lightning, but not the good kind.
    Not the kind that illuminated.
    The kind that burns.

She raised her drink like a joke, like a weapon.
He smiled.
Turned back to his conversation.

She stood there, blinking.
Thighs sticking to the too-short dress.
Shoes already hurting.
Skin already buzzing.
Heartbeat thudding too loud against ribs that never learned how to soften.

She told herself this was fun.
This was normal.
This was what people did.

She just had to hold her breath and pretend she knew the lyrics.
It wasn't the kiss.
Not really.

It was how casually he gave it.
A soft press of lips to a girl's cheek—
a throwaway gesture, light as breath,
laced in laughter and some shared joke Kaela hadn't been part of.

The girl smiled.
Tucked her hair behind one ear like it mattered.
Touched Iver's arm in that careless, familiar way.

Kaela froze.

Her drink sloshed down her wrist, but she didn't move.

Didn't breathe.
Didn't blink.

It wasn't jealousy.
It was abandonment dressed in polite party clothes.
It was the ghost of every time she'd been replaced and told not to take it personally.

He looked happy.
Effortlessly present.
And Kaela felt like she was watching him from behind ten layers of glass.

You were just last night's dopamine.
You were never going to matter this morning.

Her fingers tightened around the cup.
The plastic crackled in protest.

She downed the rest of it.
It tasted like chemicals and surrender.

Someone laughed too close to her ear.
Someone else touched her lower back.
Her body flinched like a live wire, but she smiled anyway.
Talked to someone—Marcus? Martin? Max?—and said something witty about shots.

She wasn't flirting.

She was performing.
Dragging her skeleton around in fishnets and borrowed charm.

She laughed when she was supposed to.
Let someone take a selfie with her.
Pretended she didn't see Iver dancing.
Pretended she didn't hear her heartbeat scream.

She tried to flirt with a stranger.
He told her she had cool eyeliner.
She laughed like it was the best thing anyone had ever said to her.

The lights spun harder.
The walls breathed louder.
Someone spilled something sticky across her foot and didn't say sorry.

Kaela's head swam.

She said she needed the bathroom.

No one heard her.

So she went anyway.

Alone.

Always alone.
The bathroom light buzzed like a dying fly.
Flickered once. Then steadied into a headache.

Kaela locked the door.

It didn't help.
   The noise still bled in through the walls—bass, shrieks, the rhythmic collapse of other people's joy.

She sat on the closed toilet lid.
   Held her head in both hands.

Breathed like it was a task.
   In. Out. In.
   Too fast.
   Too shallow.
   Wrong.

Her palms were sticky.
   Her thighs trembled.
   Her heart felt like it was trying to escape her ribs.

Don't cry.
   If you cry, you'll ruin the look.
   If you ruin the look, they'll see you.

Too late.

Tears burned down her cheeks.
   Mascara followed.
   Perfect skin cracked.

She stared at the mirror above the sink.
  It stared back, unsympathetic.

"You're losing him," she whispered.

Voice like broken glass.
  Fragile and sharp.

"You're too much. Again."

A sob slipped out.
  She slapped her own thigh to punish it.
  Hard enough to sting.
  Hard enough to silence it.

"You always do this," she hissed at her reflection.
  "Too loud. Too needy. You ruin everything."

*[I warned you I was too much.*
  *You didn't listen.*
  *Now you're here with me in the ugly. No edits. No filters. Just*
*impact.]*

The mirror didn't argue.

It just showed her the makeup she'd sculpted herself into, now running
like guilt.

She peeled her lashes off.
  Dropped them in the sink.
  Watched them curl like dying spiders.

She clawed her thighs.
  Short, angry scratches.
  Just enough to feel.
  Just enough to stay.

The door rattled once.
  Someone knocked.

"Occupied," she croaked.

Silence again.

She wiped her face with toilet paper.
  Blew her nose.
  Laughed—once, bitterly.

You're a fucking mess.


She stood up.
  Fixed her lipstick with shaking hands.
  Put her mask back on like armor.

Then she unlocked the door,
  stepped into the chaos again,
  and didn't look back.
  She didn't say goodbye.
  Just slipped out the door between bass drops and laughter.
  The hallway was cooler. Quieter.
  Still smelled like sweat and someone else's perfume.

Her heels dangled from one hand.

*[This is the part where most books fade to black.*
  *Not here.*
  *You don't get to look away.*
  *Not yet.]*

The footpath outside bit at her soles—pebbles, concrete cracks, traces of broken glass.
  She didn't care.
  Didn't feel it, really.

Her ears still rang.
  Her eyes burned.
  Her skin itched with leftover touch that hadn't asked for consent.

The sky was softening at the edges.
  Pale purple blooming into reluctant gold.

She walked.
  Past garbage bins, passed-out strangers, and blinking traffic lights.
  A kebab shop was just closing. A man hosed the sidewalk like it had sinned.

Kaela didn't know where she was going.
  Didn't want to.
  She just needed to not be there.

The party still echoed in her body—
  her lungs tight, her stomach hollow, her thighs tingling with self-inflicted reminders.

Every step felt like apology.
  Every breath like failure.

You're too much.
  You're always too much.


She sat on the curb.

A cat darted across the street.
  A bird shrieked like it was mocking her.
  The sunrise arrived slow and arrogant.

Kaela stared at her hands.
  Smudged lipstick on the knuckles.
  Little crescent marks from her own nails.

No one had noticed her leave.
  No one had followed.
  No one had texted.

If I disappeared, how long would it take them to realise?


She pulled her knees to her chest.
  Rested her forehead on them.
  Let the sun climb without permission.

There was no grand epiphany.

No healing.
No soundtrack swelling behind her.

Just her.

On the curb.
Alone.
Still here.

*[Still think she's dramatic?*
*Still think it's just heartbreak?*
*This is survival, babe. This is breathing through barbed wire.*
*And you're lucky you only have to read it.]*

# Seven

## Journal Entry 2

[I don't want to write metaphors today.

I don't want to be deep. or wise. or soft.

I just want to stop being a fucking punchline in someone else's healing arc.

Stop narrating me like i'm your tragic little muse.

Stop crafting my breakdowns like they're prose.

I bleed ugly.

I ache stupid.

I love recklessly and it never gets softer. only sharper.

I'm so tired of you trying to make it beautiful.

What if it's not?

What if it's just sad?

What if i'm just some girl who can't stop handing out parts of herself and calling it intimacy?

You don't get to write me soft just to make it palatable.

If you're gonna tell my story—

44

*then tell it with the teeth bared.*

*Tell it with the mascara running and the vodka breath and the stomach full of regret.*

*You wanna publish this one too?*

*Go on then. Let them see the parts you don't filter.*

*Let them choke on the real shit for once.*

*I dare you.]*

# Eight

## "They Spoke in the Language I Cried In"

It was taped to the back of a streetlight.

Crumpled, water-stained, half peeled at the corners.

Kaela only saw it because the wind caught the edge and made it flutter—like it was waving to her.

> *"Too sensitive?"*
> *"Too much?"*
> *"Come find us."*

There was no logo.

Just a time. A street. A number.

Typed in lowercase, like a whisper.

She stared at it for a long moment.

Like it might vanish if she blinked.

Like she'd imagined it into being.

Her hand moved before she could talk herself out of it.

She snapped a photo.

Stood there, barefoot in her cheap sandals, heart thudding like something sacred had just spoken.

Back at the hostel, she hovered over the number for an hour.

Typed and deleted a dozen messages.

Finally settled on:

Hey. Saw your flyer. I think I'm... one of you? Maybe.

Three dots.

Gone.

Back again.

Her stomach twisted.

Then the reply came:

Lisette here. Of course you are. You wouldn't have seen it otherwise.

Come tonight. Bring your pain. Leave your apology.

Kaela's throat went dry.

There were no instructions. No explanation.

Just an address. A time.

A door.

And something in her chest cracked open, soft and terrified.

Someone is waiting for you.

Someone believes you exist.

The house was nothing.

Peeling paint, overgrown grass, a porch light that flickered like it had opinions.

Kaela stood in front of it, heart thudding like it wanted out.

47

She knocked.

The door opened before she could second-guess herself.

Lisette.

Tall. Effortless. Wreathed in cigarette smoke and something unnameable.

Hair the colour of fuck-you confidence.

Lipstick that bled beautifully.

Eyes like she'd already read Kaela's entire soul and wasn't judging— just... intrigued.

"You're late," she said.

Then smiled.

"Which is fine. Saints always are."

Kaela blinked.

Lisette stepped aside without another word.

Inside smelled like old paper, patchouli, and rage dressed in poetry.

There were candles.

There were shadows.

There were words carved into the walls in Sharpie and lipstick and something that looked like blood.

And there were people.

A dozen, maybe more.

None of them looked like each other.

But every single one looked like her.

Fractured.

Too much.

Too quiet and too loud in the same breath.

Lisette handed her a black notebook.

"Write what you can't say," she said, "and we'll carry it for you."

Kaela took it.

Her fingers trembled.

Lisette touched her cheek.

Warm. Certain.

"You're not broken," she said.

"You're holy."

Kaela's knees buckled.

She didn't fall, but she felt it.

That inner collapse.

That tectonic shift of someone finally *believing* her pain.

She cried.

Not loud. Not ugly.

Just… quietly. Finally.

And no one told her to stop.

No chairs.

Just cushions and the thrum of silence shaped into something sacred.

They sat in a circle.

Kaela's notebook cradled in her lap like a wound.

Lisette lit a candle.

The room held its breath.

Then:

**"Speak. Bleed. Rise. Begin."**

The first girl read a poem about drowning in a family dinner.

A boy spoke of screaming into his pillow until he came.

Someone else just said, *"I want to be dead but still liked."*

No one flinched.

No one laughed.

No one offered advice.

Only the Woundkeeper—Ash—nodded. Silent. Watchful.

Their eyes shimmered like they remembered every word ever spoken in that room.

When Kaela's turn came, she didn't speak.

She just opened the notebook and held up a single page.
One sentence:

"If I have to earn love, is it still love?"

Lisette read it aloud.
Voice low. Sure.
No response was needed.
Only the sound of the candle crackling.
And the feeling—warm, eerie, terrifying—of being *understood*.
Afterwards, they didn't hug.
Didn't say *you're so brave*.
Just offered her a shared silence that felt more intimate than any words.
Kaela sat with her knees pulled to her chest.
Eyes burning.
Heart steady for the first time in months.
She was not fixed.
Not healed.
But she was... held.
Afterwards, she walked home slow.
Notebook clutched to her chest like it might fly away.
The streets blurred. The night was velvet.
She didn't cry again.
Didn't smile either.
Just floated.
When she opened the door to the hostel room, Jordan looked up from his laptop.
Headphones around his neck. One brow raised—barely.
"You alright?"
His voice was flat, neutral. Not uninterested. Just... practical.

Kaela nodded too quickly.

"Yes. Yeah."

He studied her. Not in a creepy way. Not even curious.

Just *present*.

"You look different," he said, turning back to his screen. "Quieter."

She didn't answer.

Didn't know how.

That night, she wrote for hours.

Not in her journal. In the Splinter book.

Fragments.

> *"She told me I was holy. I've never wanted to believe someone so badly."*
>
> *"If pain is a religion, I finally found my church."*
>
> *"Jordan noticed something. That scares me more than Iver ever could."*

The candle she'd stolen from the meeting flickered on her windowsill.

Her fingers were stained with ink.

Her heart ached in a new, tender place.

Not broken.

Just... renamed.

# Nine

## "Sacred Monsters"

Kaela didn't decide to go back.

Her body did.

Like gravity. Or instinct. Or faith with dirty shoes.

It moved before her brain could protest, before her logic could list the reasons she shouldn't. Before Dani's shift roster or Iver's half-smiles or the ticking clock in her chest could catch up.

The house welcomed her again like it had been waiting.

Same flickering porch light. Same sharpie-scribbled walls. Same sense that something was growing in the shadows, not mold—*meaning*.

Lisette opened the door this time with a grin and a single sentence:

*"Told you it'd feel like coming home."*

Inside, they were already gathered.

Cushions arranged in sacred disorder.

Ash sat in the center, cross-legged, notebook open on their lap like a wound that never closed.

The air shimmered with held breath and secrets not yet spoken.

Kaela sat, notebook clutched tight.

Her knees touched someone else's. No one apologized. No one pulled away.

This was a church where contact didn't mean danger—it meant you were *still here.*

Lisette lit the candle.

**"Speak. Bleed. Rise. Begin."**

A girl read about panic attacks during sex.

A boy described the time he threw his medication into the ocean and listened for applause from the waves.

Someone recited a letter they wrote to their mother and never sent—it ended with "I didn't die, but I wanted to."

And then Kaela spoke.

She hadn't planned to.

But her notebook opened on a page she didn't remember writing.

Her voice came out without permission.

> *"I smile so people don't ask if I'm drowning.*
> *And when they compliment the smile, I smile harder.*
> *Until it's the only thing I remember how to do."*

Silence.

Then—fingers snapping.

Like a forest of tiny fires igniting in the dark.

A boy near the candles whispered, "Fuck," and wiped at his eyes.

Someone mouthed *thank you.*

Lisette exhaled like a prayer had just been answered.

Kaela's skin prickled.

This was worship.

Not of God, but of *truth*, raw and unfiltered.

Here, bleeding beautifully was an art form.

Ash nodded.

Wrote something in their notebook.

Kaela didn't know what.

Didn't ask.

Afterwards, someone handed her a cup of cheap wine and a slice of orange. Communion.

Lisette leaned in, lips close to her ear, and said:

*"You were luminous."*

Kaela laughed.

A real, startled sound.

Like something inside her had been startled awake.

And somewhere in the back of her head, a voice tried to whisper: *You skipped work for this.*

She didn't hear it over the applause inside her chest.

The lipstick was Lisette's.

Technically.

But Kaela wore it now—smudged on purpose, reckless on instinct.

A red so deep it looked like it had drawn blood.

A colour that said: *I'm not soft. I'm flame.*

That said: *Look. But don't assume you understand what you're seeing.*

She'd stopped brushing her hair straight.

Let it curl, frizz, rebel.

Let it mirror her.

Her clothes changed too.

Loose tanks. Men's shirts. Jeans torn in places that looked accidental but weren't.

She stood in the bathroom mirror at the hostel, applying the lipstick slow.

Jordan passed behind her in just a towel, paused, glanced.

"You're bleeding at the mouth," he said casually, brushing his teeth.

Kaela smirked. "Perfect."

He shrugged and kept brushing.

Didn't stare. Didn't comment again.

She liked that about him. He never made her explain.

At the bar, Iver blinked when she walked in.

She was late. Not by much. Enough to notice.

"New look," he said, cocking his head.

Kaela smiled. "New me."

"You alright?"

Her smile widened. "Never better."

Lie.

She was burning.

But it felt like glory.

He smiled back, confused but charmed.

"Cool. You're glowing."

> *Glowing.*
>> *Not unraveling.*
>> *Not dancing on the edge of mania like it was a catwalk.*
>> *Glowing.*

She laughed louder than necessary. Poured drinks like rituals.

Flirted with customers. Forgot to clock out.

When she got back, the lipstick was still perfect.

She wiped it off slowly, like shedding a persona.

But underneath was the same fire.

She wrote in her Splinter book:

> *"The mirror used to lie.*
>   *Now it just exaggerates."*

Lisette spoke like a prophet drunk on her own divinity.
Every sentence felt rehearsed and holy.
Her voice didn't rise—it *swelled.*
Like it knew it was about to be quoted.
They were all sitting in the circle again.
The lights were lower.
The candle flickered like it was eavesdropping.
Lisette stood.
Red lipstick, vintage blouse, cigarette in hand despite the no-smoking sign taped to the wall.

> *"We're not sick," she said. "We're awakened. The world just isn't ready for us."*

The Splinters nodded. Drank it in.
Kaela, too.
She didn't flinch when Lisette placed a hand on her shoulder and said:

> *"You're not broken, love. You're vivid. They just haven't invented sunglasses strong enough."*

It was cheesy. It was brilliant. It made Kaela's ribs ache.
Ash sat across from them, watching.
Not smiling. Not disagreeing.
Just… observing.

As always.

Kaela read again. This time, something sharper.

> *"I wear pain like perfume.*
> *Subtle enough that you lean closer.*
> *Loud enough that it lingers when I leave."*

Finger snaps again.

A quiet gasp from someone new.

Afterwards, someone hugged her without asking.

She let it happen.

Lisette pressed a kiss to her forehead.

It wasn't maternal. It was ceremonial.

Like Kaela had been knighted.

That night, Kaela couldn't sleep.

Her heart thudded too loud in her ears.

She messaged no one.

Didn't check if Iver had texted.

Instead, she sat cross-legged on her hostel bed, whispering the line over and over like a spell:

> *"Not sick. Awakened."*

Her phone buzzed at 10:12 a.m.

Dani.

"U were rostered last night. Everything ok?"

Kaela stared at it.

Then flipped the phone over and shoved it under her pillow.

Last night, she'd been reading her soul aloud in a circle of firelight.

Last night, someone had called her divine.

Today, she was supposed to care about mojitos and table numbers?

No.

She opened her Splinter notebook instead.

Started sketching something—circles, eyes, sigils that didn't mean anything yet but *felt* true.

Iver texted next.

"Did you quit or just ghosting me? "

She didn't answer.

Couldn't.

Wouldn't.

Later that night, she saw him at the bar when she came to collect her last paycheck.

He smiled when he saw her—hesitant, hopeful.

"I've missed your weird energy," he said, handing over an envelope.

She shrugged. "You still have some."

He laughed. She didn't.

"I heard you're doing some poetry thing?"

"Something like that."

"You happy?"

Kaela tilted her head.

*"I'm real. Isn't that better?"*

He didn't know how to answer.

She didn't wait for him to try.

Back at the hostel, she curled into bed.

The notebook sat beside her like a sleeping pet.

The window hummed with Gold Coast heat and drunk girls shrieking at taxis.

Jordan was already asleep.

One arm over his eyes. Shirtless. Calm.

Kaela whispered,

*"I'm not soft. I'm sacred."*

But it didn't sound convincing.

She wrote it anyway.

## Ten

# "If They Leave, I Die"

It started with a look.

Not even a mean one. Not even sharp. Just… distant.

Like Iver had stepped three paces back inside his own head and forgotten to invite her.

She asked, "Are you okay?"

He shrugged. "Yeah. Just… you know. It's a lot sometimes."

It.

She.

Her chest went quiet—then roared.

"Right," she said, eyes fixed somewhere above his shoulder. "Too much again."

"I didn't say that."

"You didn't have to."

He sighed. The kind of sigh that comes after deciding not to argue. Not to fight.

She hated that sigh. It always came right before the vanishing.

He left.

He always did it like a gentleman—smiling, saying something kind, acting like everything was fine.

She wanted to throw something at his back just to feel real again.

Instead, she sat on her bed in the hostel, phone burning in her lap. And she texted.

Long, spiraling messages. Paragraphs shaped like pleas.

Things like:

> *"I'm sorry if I'm hard to handle. I just feel a lot."*
>
> *"You don't have to fix me. I just want you to understand."*
>
> *"I don't mean to be intense. It's just how I'm wired."*
>
> *"I know you didn't sign up for this. You probably think I'm broken."*
>
> *"Please don't go quiet. That's the worst part."*

No response.

So she sent more.

Then deleted half.

Then wrote a new one:

> *"Forget it. I'm being dramatic. Ignore me."*

Then:

> *"Actually don't ignore me. Please."*

Still nothing.

So she took a photo of herself crying—eyes wet, mouth trembling, vulnerability cranked up like a threat—and sent it.

Nothing.

Her stomach folded in on itself. She rushed to the bathroom and vomited bile into the sink.

Mascara smeared across her fingers as she wiped her face with the back of her hand.

She stared at herself in the mirror, whispering:

*"You scared him.*
*You always scare them."*

Her reflection didn't argue.

Lisette found her curled in the hostel's stairwell, back pressed to the wall, fingers trembling from the inside out.

"Iver?" she asked softly, already knowing.

Kaela just nodded.

Lisette didn't offer a hug. Didn't kneel or coo or pity.

She sat beside her like they were on a throne of ash.

*"Fuck him," she said, lighting a cigarette. "You deserve worship.*
*Not silence."*

Kaela exhaled like that was permission.

She reached into her bag and pulled out the bar napkin.

Iver's handwriting: *"Kaela—drinks on me next time. You're weird. I like it."*

She handed it to Lisette like it was a sacrificial lamb.

Lisette raised an eyebrow. "This it?"

Kaela nodded.

They walked to the Splinter house. No words. Just ritual in motion.

In the centre of the cracked coffee table, the Woundkeeper lit a candle without asking why.

Lisette dropped the napkin into the dish.

Flames caught fast. The ink blistered, curling like regret.

Kaela watched it burn. Didn't flinch. Didn't cry.

Lisette reached into her purse and pulled out a lipstick tube—
*Stigmata Red.*

*"You need new armour,"* she said, unscrewing the cap.

Kaela tilted her chin up.

Lisette painted her mouth like anointing a saint.

*"We're not sick," she whispered. "We're awakened."*

Kaela felt the wax soak into her skin like gospel.

*Maybe I'm not broken. Maybe I'm just misread*
*—holy in the wrong dialect.*

She didn't say it aloud.

Lisette already knew.

She posted a fragment first.

Just five words from her journal:

*"I don't know my edges."*

No context. No hashtags. Just raw bone on a glowing screen.

The likes began immediately.

She watched them roll in while lying on her back in the lounge of
the Splinter house, one bare foot pressed against the wall like it was
holding her there.

*"You okay?"*
*"Same."*

*"Fuck, I felt this."*

She posted again.

*"I bled too pretty for him to care."*

More hearts. More comments.
Each one landed like morphine—small, warm, numbing.
Her pain, finally seen. Filtered. Framed. Consumed.
She sipped wine Lisette had poured into a chipped teacup.
It tasted like spoiled cherries and false promises.

*Maybe I don't need him to reply.*
*Maybe I just need to be wanted in pixels.*

She opened her contacts. Scrolled. Found his name.
Deleted it.
Then, thirty seconds later, added it back.

*Iver.*

Then deleted it again.
Then added it six more times under different spellings:
"Iver," "Iverrr," "DON'T TEXT," "He Doesn't Care," "STOP IT," "Iver.
Again."
She hit record. Whispered:
"Please miss me back."
Then deleted it before it could exist.
She laughed once, bitter and breathless, then went silent.
Lisette handed her a Sharpie and a napkin.

Kaela scrawled the word *"hollow"* and pinned it to the fridge with a magnet shaped like a skull.

Art. Always art.

Even pain had to be curated.

Even numbness needed a frame.

The house went quiet. That thick kind of quiet, like everyone was pretending not to feel.

In the next room, someone was playing a soft cover of a loud song. A girl wept openly in the hallway. No one stopped her. This was the kind of place where pain didn't get fixed—it got witnessed.

Kaela lay on the floor of the lounge, cheek pressed against cool tile. Mascara smudged into her jawline like war paint applied by a ghost.

Her phone lay face-down on her chest. No notifications. No vibrations. No him.

She'd set the screen saver to black. It made it easier to imagine it was off. Easier to lie.

Her fingers twitched toward it. Then stopped.

In the kitchen, someone—maybe Jordan—moved quietly. Cabinets opened. Closed. Water ran.

She didn't look.

But she knew.

Jordan had a way of *not looking at her* that still felt like care.

He didn't ask where she'd been.

He never did.

He just existed nearby like a lighthouse: steady, wordless, unmoved.

She turned her face to the ceiling and whispered Iver's name. Once. Soft. Like a child calling for a dream to return.

The word cracked in her mouth.

The Splinters lit candles in the next room. She heard Lisette's voice like a sermon on fire:

*"We do not die for love.*
   *We resurrect in its absence."*

The group screamed together, feral and cathartic.
   Kaela didn't scream.
   She just listened.
   Because not screaming—*choosing* silence—felt like control.
   And she needed control more than she needed air.

They didn't say goodbye.
   They just stopped replying.
   And that's the thing—
   I don't die loud.
   I die unnoticed.

**Eleven**

# Journal Entry 3

⚜

*I didn't scream.*

*Not because I'm strong.*

*Not because I'm healed.*

*Because I didn't want anyone to hear it and mistake it for drama.*

*There's this ache in my ribs that feels like a missed call.*

*Like someone almost loved me and then remembered why they shouldn't.*

*I know the difference between solitude and abandonment.*

*This is abandonment with better lighting.*

*I keep thinking I should be proud of myself for walking away.*

*But I didn't walk.*

*I crumpled slowly and called it growth.*

*I want to be wanted. Not tolerated. Not endured.*

*Wanted like a storm is wanted—because it's terrifying and still necessary.*

*And yet here I am. Again.*

*Writing down everything I wish I could say out loud.*

*Wishing I could post it without a filter.*

*Wishing I didn't check for likes like they're defibrillators.*

*[You still reading this? Still romanticising it?*
*Good.*
*Now sit in the quiet with me.*
*No music. No metaphor. Just ache.]*

# Twelve

## "We Were Never Built for Stability"

Kaela stood in the centre of the circle, barefoot, smudged in red lipstick like war paint. Not hers—Lisette's. Always Lisette's.

But tonight, the room listened to her.

The candles hissed as if in reverence. Pages crackled. Ash floated like snow from old gods.

She read from her journal like it was scripture.
Eyes closed. Voice steady. A whisper made of knives:

"I was not born for calm.
I was carved for collapse."

A moan rippled through the room—raw, aching, holy.

The Splinters clutched their cups tighter. Mila wiped tears with her sleeve.

Even Ash, silent and granite-eyed, nodded once.

Kaela felt it bloom in her chest.

Power.

Not control—not safety.

But influence. The drug of being seen and swallowed whole.

They quoted her now.

Wrote her fragments in chalk on alley walls.

Painted her words in blood-red ink across mirror shards.

She started calling herself Priestess of Pain like it was a title she earned.

Lisette didn't correct her. Just watched with the expression of a woman watching a younger version of herself dancing toward fire.

Kaela barely slept.

She didn't need to. Not when attention buzzed louder than caffeine, louder than memory, louder than grief.

Every night bled into the next.

And she was high on it all.

Until the door opened.

And the new one stepped in.

He moved like a storm had dressed itself in skin.

Hair like dusk.
  Eyes like lit cigarettes.
  The air changed when he walked through it.

Nate.

Kaela's lips parted before she meant to speak.
  But he didn't look at her—not yet.

Lisette leaned in close, whisper-biting:

"Don't fall for his kind.
  They'll see you, sure.
  But only the parts you haven't forgiven."

Kaela turned her head slowly, a smile blooming like something feral.

"Too late."

Because when his eyes did find hers—
  It wasn't like being noticed.

It was like being recognized.
  And that was far more dangerous.
  Nate didn't speak much that first night.

Didn't need to.

He sat just outside the circle's heat—leaning back on his elbows, legs sprawled like he owned the floor beneath him.

His journal stayed closed. His mouth, too.

But his presence—that was loud.

Kaela tried not to look.

Failed.

Tried again.

Failed better.

He had the kind of face that made you think about the parts of yourself you swore you'd healed.

Not beautiful. Not soft.

But true in the way wounds are true.

When Lisette lit the candle for confessions, Kaela usually led.

That night, she hesitated.

"Someone else want to start?"

No one moved.

Until Nate stood.

His journal still closed.

He stepped into the light like he wasn't afraid to burn.

Smiled once. Crooked. Empty.

"I don't write shit down.
  I remember everything I regret."


Silence.
  Even Ash blinked.

Then, he spoke:

"I kissed my best friend's girl.
  Told her I'd never lie.
  Then I left the country instead."


A beat. Another.

"I liked the way her heart broke.
  It looked like mine."


He sat down again like nothing happened.

Kaela felt her ribs pull tight around her lungs.

Red flag. Bright. Waving.
  And yet.

She smiled at him across the circle.
  He didn't smile back.
  Just raised one brow, as if to say: You too?

Later, she found him on the porch.
  Smoking something cheap.
  No shoes. No shame.

"You're intense," she said, arms crossed against the breeze.

He exhaled smoke through his nose like a dragon tired of pretending it wasn't real.

"You're fluorescent," he said. "Most people dim to survive."

Kaela swallowed.

"Maybe I don't want to survive.
  Maybe I want to detonate."

Nate flicked ash into the dark.

"Then let's see what your ruin looks like."

And just like that—

the match was lit.

The next meeting, she wore red.

Not Lisette's shade—deeper, bloodier.
  A color that dared anyone to look away.

Kaela sat closer to Nate now.
  Close enough to feel the static between them, like their atoms recognized each other's bad decisions.

He didn't flirt.
  Didn't charm.
  Just observed her like a piece of poetry he didn't trust, but couldn't stop reading.

Lisette raised her eyebrows once. Said nothing.

Kaela read another fragment aloud, her voice half-moan, half-manifesto:

"I am a cathedral built from all the times I wasn't loved back."


A collective inhale.
  Someone whispered "fuck" under their breath.

She glanced sideways—
  Nate wasn't clapping like the others.
  He just tilted his head.

"You believe that?" he asked, low and slow.

Kaela shrugged. "Some days."

"And the other days?"

"I rewrite it prettier."

He smirked.

"Pretty lies are still lies."

She leaned in, heartbeat thick in her throat. "That's the point."

He laughed once—short, like he didn't mean to.

"You're not built for stability, Kaela."

"Neither are you."

Their hands didn't touch.

But her pulse galloped anyway.

—

Later, in the kitchen, she found lipstick smeared on the edge of her teacup.
Not hers. Lisette's.

A silent warning. Or a dare.
Kaela kissed the rim and took a sip.

If she was going to burn,
she wanted the whole fucking city to smell it.
The Splinters gathered on the beach that night.

No candles. No scripts.
Just moonlight sharp enough to slit the sky and the roar of saltwater that didn't care who they were.

Kaela walked barefoot over cold sand, the kind that numbs you before it heals.
She wore black. Lipstick like fresh war.
Nate followed three steps behind, quiet, volatile, eyes full of unsaid things.

Ash drew a circle in the sand with their heel.
Lisette lit a single match and let it burn down to her fingers.

"Tonight, no lies," she said. "No metaphors. No edits."

Kaela stepped into the circle.
  Looked straight at Nate and said:

"I want to be worshipped until I forget why I ever needed it."

No one flinched. Not here. Not in this place where pain was holy.

Nate stepped in next.
  Rolled up his sleeve. Showed the scar on his wrist like a relic.

"I want to stop testing people to see if they'll leave."

Lisette kissed the sand between them.

"This is the beginning of the unraveling."

—

After, Kaela and Nate walked home in silence.
  The air smelled like seaweed and hunger.

Outside the hostel, he paused.
  Lit a cigarette. Didn't offer her one.

"You're burning out," he said. "Fast."

She smiled, too tired to lie.

"Good. I'd rather explode than fade."

He exhaled smoke toward the moon.

"You will.
    And you'll look divine doing it."

She didn't ask him up.
    He wouldn't have come.

But when she looked over her shoulder and said,

"I'll see you,"

He replied:

"Yeah. You will."

And when she lay in bed that night,
    sweat sticking her to the sheets,
    her skin still buzzing from ritual and rawness—

she didn't think about Iver.
  Not even once.

She dreamed of fire,
  and woke up smiling.

# Thirteen

## Journal Entry 4

*I said i didn't think about him.*
  *and maybe that was true.*
  *For a minute.*
  *For a night.*
  *For the space between nate's eyes and the ocean bleeding silver.*
  *But now?*
  *Now i can't stop wondering who i am when no one's quoting me.*
  *When the beach is empty and the sand's just sand.*
  *Not sacred. not symbolic.*
  *Just cold and in my shoes.*
  *They worshiped me tonight.*
  *I said something sharp, and they snapped their fingers like it meant*
*something.*
  *Nate looked at me like i was the punchline to a prophecy.*
  *and i felt—*
  *Fuck, i felt so alive.*
  *But now i'm just*

*awake.*

*And empty.*

*And too aware of the silence between text notifications.*

*I keep refreshing shit that isn't going to change.*

*Keep pretending this notebook is a confessional instead of a trap.*

*I said i wanted to be worshipped until i forgot why i needed it.*

*But the truth is*

*I want to be loved so gently*

*i forget how loud i get.*

*I want someone to see the parts i don't post.*

*The collapse without metaphors.*

*The crying that doesn't sound pretty.*

*I'm tired of playing priestess.*

*I want to be held.*

*Not reverently.*

*Just... actually.*

# Fourteen

## "Someone Always Falls"

It wasn't love. It was ignition. A holy, feral kind of combustion.

Kaela and Nate didn't kiss—they collided. Their mouths found each other like secrets too dangerous to keep buried. There was no sweetness, no seduction—just need. Desperate, clawing, sacred need. Her hands fisted in the fabric of his shirt, nails digging into the muscle beneath. His teeth grazed her collarbone like he was hungry for the pieces of her no one else dared to touch.

They didn't bother with the bed. First time was against the wall in the laundry room of the hostel—his belt halfway undone, her shirt yanked off so fast one of the buttons screamed and surrendered. Her bra hung from a pipe like a white flag. He didn't ask permission. He knew. Knew where her body hummed, where her pulse surged, where her shame began and ended. He touched her like a prophecy.

She yanked his shirt off over his head. Sculpted. Scarred. Godlike in the way only broken men can be—stitched together with failure and still standing. His cock pressed hard through denim—hot, insistent, aching with promise. She dropped to her knees like she'd found an altar, hands firm on his thighs, eyes locked on his. Took him in like devotion. He groaned, one hand braced on the washer, the other tangled in her damp hair, holding, trembling, praising.

They fucked like heathens in the Sunday sun. Quick. Vicious. Divine.

Later, curled in the corner, breath still hitching, she traced the scar across his chest with reverent fingers.

"Who gave you this one?"

"Me."

No shame. No explanation. Just the fact of it, and that was enough.

That was the rule between them: pain didn't need a backstory.
  Trauma was an accent, not a monologue.

When they made it to an actual bed, it wasn't softer. It was just horizontal.

He whispered things against her throat like mantras—

"You're more than human."

"I'd let you destroy me."
"Say my name like it's the last word you'll ever speak."

And she did. Loud. Brazen. Like a hymn soaked in gasoline.

The wall thudded. The lights flickered. Her body lit up like ritual.

And for a moment—just a moment—she was everything.

\*\*\*

The message hit the Splinters group chat like a detonation:

"Has anyone seen Mika?"

Then another.

"He's gone."

Then the gut-punch:

"He left a note."

Lisette was the one who read it aloud.

Her voice didn't crack—it fractured. Subtle, sharp.

"Kaela made me feel like I was worth burning for.
  I wish I could've survived the fire."

The room went silent.

Not reverent silence. Not contemplative.

Accusatory.

Ash shut their eyes. Mila sobbed into the crook of her arm. Someone across the room hurled their journal into the wall. Pages scattered like dead wings, flapping with grief.

Kaela froze. Rigid. A statue sculpted in guilt.

Lisette didn't look at her. Didn't point. Just said:

"This isn't performance.
  It's people."

And Kaela—suddenly hollow, suddenly orphaned from her own voice—walked out without a word.

—

She didn't sleep for two days.

Didn't eat. Didn't write. Didn't scroll.

Jordan knocked once. Left a water bottle by the door. No questions. No comments. Just presence.

She lay under her bedsheet like a chalk outline. Mascara-streaked. Sweat-soaked. Breathing like it hurt. Every time she blinked, she saw Mika's face. His clapping hands. His eyes during her poem, glinting like someone who believed.

"Kaela made me feel worth burning for."

The words repeated like scripture carved into her lungs.

She whispered his name into the pillow.
    He didn't answer.

The hostel was too quiet. Or maybe just too loud in all the wrong places.

She scratched lines into her journal that didn't make sense.
    Crossed them out.
    Ripped the page.
    Burned it.

—

On the third day, she posted.

A photo of waves crashing under a thundercloud.

Captioned it with a poem. Sharp. Unapologetic:

"If you loved the spark,
   don't cry about the fire.
   I never promised warmth.
   Only light."

The likes hit fast. Heart emojis. Fire gifs. Comments about "power" and "truth."

Some praised her. Called her a goddess. A saint of pain.

Some blocked her. Called her dangerous. Selfish. A trigger in lipstick.

Lisette said nothing.

Nate messaged her one line:

"You still shine. Just be careful what you illuminate."

Kaela lay in bed, sheets kicked off, one thigh still sticky with the sweat of insomnia.

The guilt hadn't left.
   But neither had the hunger.

She wanted to be worshiped.
   Even if it meant becoming the altar and the flame.


—

## Fifteen

# Journal Entry 5

*I should've shut up.*

*I should've kept my fucking poems to myself.*

*Who the hell do i think i am?*

*What gave me the right to bleed in public like it was a blessing?*

*He's dead.*

*And i'm still here.*

*Posting. Posing.*

*Putting my lipstick on like it's not war paint smeared with someone else's ashes.*

*Everyone saw the note.*

*His last breath had my name in it.*

*Like i handed him the match.*

*Like i was the fire and the reason he stepped into it.*

*You don't get to be a prophet if someone dies believing you.*

*You don't get to write the pretty lines and call it healing when the ink still smells like smoke.*

*I think i killed him.*

*Not with my hands—*
*But with my voice.*
*My spotlight.*
*My stupid, hollow hunger to be understood.*
*I keep thinking if i'd just told him he mattered.*
*Or smiled longer.*
*Or sat closer.*
*Or shut the fuck up for once and listened instead of performing—*
*Maybe he'd still be breathing.*
*Maybe this wouldn't feel like my funeral too.*
*I don't want your pity.*
*I don't want your comments or your claps or your fucking aesthetic grief.*
*I want him back.*
*But he's ash now.*
*And i'm still here.*
*Writing.*
*Like that'll fix anything.*

**[You still reading this? what's next—you gonna turn this into merch?]**
**[make sure the font looks cute when you crucify me.]**

## Sixteen

# "The Gospel According to Me"

Kaela hadn't slept. Again.

The page glared at her like it knew her secrets. She wrote anyway. Not a poem. Not a line fragment. A doctrine. Her own gospel.

"Pain is the holiest language.

Attention is the prayer.

If no one hears you bleed, did you even exist?"

The Splinters worshipped every word. Lisette reposted it with the caption: "This is divine." Kaela felt it bloom inside her like a cancer made of glitter. Every share, every quote, every comment—it lit up her bones like hallelujahs.

She was becoming something else now. Not a girl. Not even a woman. A warning. A psalm. A monument carved from ache.

—

And then—Jordan walked out of the shower.

Naked. Casual. Damp hair plastered to his forehead. Towel tossed over one shoulder like a suggestion, not a necessity.

Kaela looked up from her laptop. Paused. Visibly recalculated her entire sense of self.

He was... sculpted. Not gym-bro sculpted. Not vanity sculpted. Just— functional. Dense. Solid. Every line defined by a life of tension and control.

And he was hung. Like... unfairly so. Like a Greek statue had quietly evolved and started taking ADHD meds.

*[NOPE. NO WAY.*
  *DELETE THIS.*
  *WHY IS THIS STILL HERE?*
  *WHY ARE YOU—*
  *YOU'RE STILL READING?!*
  *Oh my God. I'm going to haunt your Google search history.*
  *I SWEAR I WROTE THAT IN A MOMENT OF HORMONAL COLLAPSE.*
  *Can you at least pretend you didn't just picture it?*
  *Disrespectful.]*

Her brain skipped like a scratched CD.

He didn't even notice. Or, worse, he did notice and didn't care. He glanced at her once—eyes clinical, neutral, polite as a Danish waiter.

"Morning." "You're not wearing anything." "Neither were you last week," he said, shrugging. "Fair's fair."

She blushed. Immediately hated herself for it.

He moved to the sink, casually brushing his teeth like his cock wasn't a full narrative arc.

"You're not embarrassed?" she asked. "Should I be?"

Foam in his mouth. Completely unfazed.

"It's a body. Yours isn't a secret, why should mine be?"

She bit the inside of her cheek.

"Still. You could at least—cover it?" "You didn't." "I was melting." "And I'm clean. Now we're even."

She turned back to her laptop but couldn't stop thinking about how absolutely composed he was. Like shame wasn't even in his vocabulary.

And for a flash—just a flicker of envy—she wanted that. She also hated how symmetrical his collarbones were.

Jordan finished brushing, tossed the towel on his bed like a throw pillow. As he turned to grab his clothes, Kaela blinked once, then muttered:

"Hvordan falder du ikke over den der…"
  (How do you not trip over that thing…)

Not loud. Just to herself. But loud enough for the walls to smirk.

And maybe—just maybe—Jordan heard it. Because his mouth twitched, the barest ghost of a smirk. But he didn't look back. Didn't give her the satisfaction.

She clenched her jaw, cheeks pink and thoughts spiraling. He started dressing. Still casual. Still unbothered.

Kaela closed her laptop too hard.

"Must be nice." "What?" "Walking around like the world didn't hurt you."

He looked at her then. Really looked. Like he was reading her footnotes in real time.

"It did," he said softly. "I just don't need it to like me back."

And then he left the room. And she hated how much sense that made.

—

She couldn't stop.

She knew the crash was coming—could feel it stalking her—but the attention was a drug with no comedown.

Every comment, every "I relate," every crying-face emoji on her posts— it fed her like communion.

She wasn't Kaela anymore.
  She was The Saint.
  The one who made pain beautiful.
  The one who bled in stanzas and walked like fire was a second skin.

At night, Nate would hold her hips like they were prayer beads, mutter her own lines into her ear like scripture.

"You make hurting look holy."
  "You make me forget I ever wanted to get better."

She shook under him, mouth open, brain boiling.

And then she'd roll over, face the wall, and cry into the pillow while he slept.

Because no one wanted the quiet version of her. The boring one. The soft one. The girl who just wanted to be held without needing to earn it.

She started skipping Splinter meetings unless she was leading.
  Started checking how many reposts she got before she even opened her messages.

One night, she stared at her reflection and whispered:

"Who the fuck even are you anymore?"

The mirror didn't answer. It just smirked.

Behind her, Jordan spoke, voice low and even:

"I know what it's like. To be the version of yourself that gets clapped for... and not the one that actually needs help."

She didn't respond. Just blinked.

He walked past, brushing her shoulder, and added:

"They love your echo, Kaela. Not your voice."

And then he shut the door behind him.

She stood there for a long time, mascara half-melted, heart aching.

And for the first time in weeks—

She wanted to be quiet.

*[AND HERE COMES THE "POETIC COMEDOWN."*
*Cue the soft music. Dim the lights. Let the readers feel deep without actually doing anything about it.*
*Well guess what?*
*I'm still here.*
*Still bleeding for your catharsis.*
*Still tap-dancing for empathy points while you sip your oat milk lattes and highlight your favourite trauma lines.*
*Enjoy the show, I guess.]*

## Seventeen

# Journal Entry – Jordan

*I'm not a writer. Not like her.*

*But I need to put this somewhere.*

*Sometimes I think Kaela burns just to see who'll pull her out of the fire.*

*And I keep jumping in like I won't drown.*

*She doesn't ask for help. She broadcasts ache like it's a performance art piece, and I'm the janitor sweeping up the aftermath.*

*I don't mind.*

*I mean, I do.*

*But I won't stop.*

*Because someone needs to stay sane. Someone needs to have two feet on the ground while she tries to walk the ceiling.*

*She makes me feel invisible sometimes.*

*Not in a cruel way—just... background. Set dressing for her chaos.*

*The lighthouse, right? The one that doesn't move. The one that doesn't get rescued.*

*Just keeps glowing.*

*I don't need applause.*

But some days, I wish she'd look at me the way she looks at the people who hurt her.

Like I matter.

Like I'm dangerous.

Instead, I'm safe.

And safe people don't get written about.

So I write this. Quietly.

To remind myself that I exist, too.


[oh my god JORDAN.]

[you absolute fucking lighthouse.]

[i'm sorry you feel like furniture in my opera. i'm sorry i forgot lighthouses get tired too.]

[you think i don't see you, but i do. i watch you—not like a firework, but like a faultline.]

[you think safety is boring? maybe it is. but it's also the first thing i crave when i stop performing.]

[so no—you don't get written about like the others.]

[you get written with. in the quiet. in the pauses. in the breath between stanzas.]

[i don't burn at you. i orbit you.]

[that has to mean something.]

## Eighteen

# "You're My Everything Until You're Not"

Nate said something—offhand, nothing. But it lodged in her ribs like glass.

Maybe it was the way he looked at his phone while she spoke. Maybe it was the way he didn't touch her shoulder after sex. Maybe it was just that he wasn't hurting loud enough to match her volume.

So she said it.

"You only love me when I'm bleeding."

He flinched. Laughed bitterly.

"You only feel loved when someone's bleeding for you."

And just like that, she ignited.

Words flew like shards. She accused. He deflected. She cried. He froze.

"You're not a person," she hissed. "You're a trigger warning in tight jeans."

He left without slamming the door. That hurt more. Silence is a sharper blade than shouting.

Two days. Three. No messages. No updates in the Splinters chat. She told herself he was just being dramatic. That she didn't care.

But her hands started shaking whenever her phone lit up. She couldn't eat. Couldn't write. She went to Dusk but forgot how to flirt. Forgot how to stand. Iver wasn't working. Dani gave her a once-over and just said, "Go home."

Kaela didn't go home.

She found a bar. New. Loud. Full of strangers. She let a guy buy her three drinks. He looked nothing like Nate. That helped. His name was—fuck, maybe it was Matt. Maybe Max.

The stranger didn't matter.

He'd bought her a drink. Said something smooth and stupid. She'd laughed too hard. Let him press her against a wall behind the bar near the staff exit. His hands were eager, unskilled, forgettable. She'd closed her eyes and let his mouth wander, pretending he was someone else. Anyone else. Nate. The version of Nate she'd built in her head before the silences.

It wasn't good. It wasn't terrible either. It just was.

A human-shaped distraction. A gasp to keep the sob from coming.

When it ended, he muttered something like "You're wild" and zipped his jeans with one hand. She didn't answer. Just smoothed her skirt and walked away, not looking back.

She found the bar's toilet—cold, pink-lit, and lined with cracked mirrors that made every reflection a little warped. Kaela locked the door. Stared at herself. Mascara haloed under her eyes. Lipstick smeared like a bad punchline. Her neck was blotched with fingerprints. Her mouth felt alien.

She dropped onto the closed toilet seat, pulling her knees to her chest.

"You're not in love," she whispered to the fluorescent light above. "You're just addicted to the idea of being someone's everything."

*[AND YOU—READER, AUTHOR, WHOEVER THE FUCK IS STILL LINGERING—DON'T YOU DARE NOD ALONG LIKE THIS MAKES SENSE TO YOU.*
*This is my spiral. My script.*
*Not some relatable Pinterest quote for your heartbreak mood board.*
*Go ahead. Try to turn this into art too.*
*God, you people will eat anything if it bleeds pretty enough.]*

A beat.

Her phone buzzed in her bag. She didn't check it. Just rested her forehead on her knees and breathed through the ache.

This wasn't about the boy she just fucked. It wasn't even about Nate, not entirely.

It was about the chasm that opened when he vanished. About how she tried to fill it with bodies and poetry and eyeliner so sharp it could puncture skin. About the terror that maybe—just maybe—she wasn't enough for anyone to stay.

"He's gone," she told the empty room. "You scared him off."

Another buzz. Probably a meme in the hostel group chat. Or Lisette. Or silence. She couldn't decide which would be worse.

She wiped her face with the scratchy toilet paper. Fixed her hair in the mirror. She saw three Kaelas in the cracked mirror. All of them wrong.

The girl looking back at her was still there. Still standing. Still cracked—but symmetrical enough to pass inspection.

Kaela flushed nothing. Washed her hands like she was cleansing the memory. Opened the door. Stepped out.

And walked straight into the sound of music too loud, laughter too forced, and a world that hadn't noticed she'd gone missing for a while.

Kaela woke up with no memory of getting back to the hostel. She called it a cry for attention.

Lisette called it performance art.

The truth? Kaela wasn't sure what the hell it was.

One and a half blister packs of anti-anxiety meds. Washed down with vodka in the middle of the afternoon while everyone else in the hostel was laughing about some goddamn group surf lesson. She hadn't even wanted to die. Not really. She just wanted out. Out of her own head. Out of her own skin. Just… out.

She'd texted Lisette a line from a Sylvia Plath poem.

Lisette sent back three heart emojis and a skull.

No one called. No one knocked. No one came.

Kaela lay on her side for an hour, head spinning, thoughts like broken record skips.

"You're so dramatic." "You're always the center of your own suffering." "You turned your breakdown into a fucking monologue."

She imagined what the Splinters would say if she told them. Some would call it brave. Some would say she was attention-seeking. Most wouldn't say anything at all. They'd just quote her on Instagram and call it healing.

Her stomach ached. Her fingers were numb. But she didn't throw up. She didn't black out. She just existed in that unbearable grey between almost and nothing.

When Jordan came home that night, she was already back in bed. Fully dressed. Hair washed. No smudged makeup. No visible proof.

He paused in the doorway, sensing it—whatever it was.

"You okay?"

She gave him the default.

"Fine."

A long beat. Then he walked over to his bed. Tossed his bag. Sat down.

"You don't have to lie to me, you know."

"I'm not."

"Okay."

He didn't press. Didn't demand. Just lay back on his pillow, arms crossed behind his head, staring at the ceiling like it held all the answers.

Kaela wanted to scream at him. Thank him. Break him open just to see if something inside him bled like hers did.

Instead, she curled tighter under the blanket.

"It wasn't serious," she whispered.

"What wasn't?"

"What I almost did."

A breath.

"Good."

"It was just a performance."

Another pause.

"Still scared me."

She flinched at that.

"You weren't even here."

"Doesn't mean I wasn't worried."

She turned away from him, cheeks burning.

Because that—that one line—meant more than a hundred apologies from Nate or a thousand flame-reacts from strangers on her poetry posts.

She bit her knuckle to keep from crying.

The Splinters loved her for her pain.

Jordan just wanted her alive.

And somehow... that felt worse.

Her shoes were still on. Her phone was under her thigh, screen cracked slightly—probably from the bathroom floor. A single text blinked on the lock screen from Lisette: "You okay?" Not "Are you alive?" Not "Where are you?"

Just that sterile, lukewarm concern wrapped in casual grammar.

"Yeah," she texted back. "All good :D "

The emoji made her want to puke.

Her throat burned—cheap vodka, bile, the raw scrape of words never said. She hadn't cried last night. Not properly. Not when she should've. Now her chest ached from holding it all in like a breath stretched too far.

She sat up slowly. Her body was stiff. Her thighs ached. The stranger hadn't even taken off her underwear, just moved it aside. She couldn't remember his name. Didn't want to.

"It didn't mean anything," she told herself aloud. "It wasn't about Nate."

It was always about Nate.

The morning light through the floral curtains was offensive. Everything looked like it was trying too hard to be soft. As if pastels could soften the bite of self-loathing.

Jordan's bed was empty. Probably at the beach. Or the kitchen. Or off existing like a perfectly tuned algorithm of calm. She hated how stable he seemed. Hated that he didn't crumble with her. That he didn't need to be seen to feel real.

She stood. Stripped. Stepped into the shower and let the cold water hit her like a slap.

A line whispered in her head, uninvited:

"Stop using my pain to write your art."

Nate's voice, still sharp behind her ribs. He'd sent it in response to her last message—a photo of her face streaked in tears with a captioned poem that wasn't subtle. She'd thought it was raw. He'd thought it was manipulative.

Maybe it was both.

"I'm sorry," she had texted back.

But he hadn't replied.

She leaned her head against the tiles. Felt the tremble in her knees and told herself it was just the cold.

Her fingers curled around the soap but didn't move. She didn't scrub. Didn't wash. Just stood there and let the chill gnaw at her skin until it felt like something was being earned. Like penance. Or clarity.

Eventually, she stepped out. Didn't dry off. Just stood dripping on the mat, staring at her own reflection again.

"You're fine," she told the mirror.

"You're always fine."

She got dressed like she was suiting up for war. Clothes loud enough to distract. Eyeliner sharp enough to maim. Lips cherry-red and defiant.

The performance was back on.

And no one—not Lisette, not Nate, not Jordan—would get to see the cracks underneath.

Not today.

## Nineteen

# Journal: "Untitled / Unwritten"

I tried.
  I fucking tried.

> ~~You loved me like a lesson~~
> ~~I bled like a badge~~
> ~~We fucked like forgiveness~~
> ~~but no one was forgiven~~
> ~~You said my name like a warning~~
> ~~I wore yours like a scar~~
> ~~We collapsed on purpose~~
> ~~because healing was too quiet~~
> ~~I'm not your art~~
> ~~I'm not your altar~~
> ~~I'm not~~
> ~~I'm not~~
> ~~I'm~~

Fuck it.

   Forget it.

   Maybe some wounds don't rhyme.

   – K

*[you happy now? you made me leave this in. bet you're framing it like it's brave. it's not. it's just broken.]*

# Twenty

## "Too Much Skin, Not Enough Self"

❧

Kaela stood in front of the mirror again. Not the clean one in the bathroom, not the one Jordan used with that obnoxiously neutral face while brushing his teeth like he was made of calm.

This one—the cracked sliver of glass next to the lockers, the one that split her down the middle every time she dared to look too long.

She didn't recognize the girl staring back. And not in the poetic, abstract way. She genuinely couldn't place the version of herself she was performing.

Lisette's lipstick. Ava's cadence. The way she leaned into conversations with her head tilted like Rumi did. Even her posture was stolen— shoulders rolled back in performative confidence, mimicking how the new Splinter boy sat like he was always one moment from levitating.

Kaela was a collage. A magpie of identities.

And it was working.

She got praise. Reposts. A quote from her gospel was now the pinned post on three different Splinter accounts. They called her Saint Kaela now—half in jest, half in awe. She was holy in her damage. She was what they wanted to become: proof that pain could be powerful.

But it didn't feel powerful. It felt fucking hollow.

Every time someone said, "You saved me," she wanted to ask, "Then why do I still feel like I'm drowning?"

The room spun in quiet waves. Too many nights without sleep. Too many days pushing through without food because her stomach rebelled against everything except coffee and other people's attention.

She hadn't written anything real in weeks. Not her own words. Just curated fragments—pain arranged like flowers in a funeral display. Beautiful. Grief-struck. Stale.

The cracked mirror flickered with movement. Jordan. Back from his run. Shirtless, headphones around his neck, that cursed easy grace that made her want to throw things. Not out of attraction. Out of jealousy.

He knew who he was. He didn't need an audience to believe in his own gravity.

She turned away, but not fast enough. He caught her. His eyes flicked over her reflection, then landed on the fresh welt on her upper arm. Hidden beneath bracelets. But the angle had exposed it.

His expression didn't change. That made it worse.

"You okay?"

"Fine."

Jordan walked over. Sat on his bunk. Waited. Not a therapist. Not a hero. Just... there.

"You're starting to wear other people's ghosts."

She blinked.

"What?"

"You talk like Lisette now. You move like Rumi. You don't even blink like yourself anymore."

Kaela crossed her arms, voice tight.

"So?"

"So I liked the Kaela who stared too long but didn't say anything. The one who had opinions and didn't always need to bleed to prove them."

She laughed—sharp and brittle.

"Well, congrats, you're the only one."

"That's not true."

"Really? Where are the others then? Where's Nate? Where's Lisette? Where the fuck is anyone when I'm not interesting anymore?"

Jordan didn't respond. He just looked at her. Still. Firm. Unshaken.

"You need real help. Not just pain dressed as poetry."

That landed like a slap.

"Fuck you."

"No. Fuck this whole cult of collapse you've built. Fuck the fact that people only clap for you when you're on fire. That's not healing. That's codependency with your own suffering."

Kaela took a step back like she'd been hit.

"You're just jealous you don't get it. You're boring. You don't feel like we do."

Jordan's jaw tightened.

"Don't confuse my calm for emptiness."

He stood. Gathered his things. Didn't slam the door. Didn't even look back.

That hurt more than anything.

That night, she carved again. Not deep. Just enough. The knife was clean. The strokes precise. Controlled. It wasn't about pain. It was about quiet.

She didn't post about it. Didn't perform it. It was hers.

She sat on the floor, headphones in, letting the dull roar of rain sounds drown out her thoughts. Her journal was open beside her, untouched. Not even fragmented words this time.

She hated silence now. Silence reminded her of herself.

Every sound in the hostel grated: someone coughing, another giggling through a late-night phone call, the hum of the vending machine that no one ever used.

Jordan's bunk stayed empty. He didn't return.

She slept in her clothes. When the sun came up, it made her feel transparent.

\*\*\*

Kaela took the mirror off the wall.

It had always been a cursed object. It knew too much. Showed too much.

She set it on the floor, sat cross-legged, and stared at herself in the fractured glass.

"Who are you when no one's looking?"

She whispered it like a dare.

The girl in the mirror looked tired. Older. Worn. The bruises beneath her eyes weren't poetic. They were malnutrition, insomnia, dehydration. Consequences.

She held up a tube of Lisette's lipstick. Applied it perfectly. A mask. A costume.

Then wiped it off with the back of her hand.

"That's not me."

The cracks in the mirror caught the light like a halo of brokenness. Her crown of thorns.

"Pain is the holiest language."

"Bullshit."

Kaela stood. Wrapped the mirror in a towel. Walked downstairs.

Outside, the bins were full. Overflowing with cheap fast food and stale beer. She propped the mirror beside them.

Let someone else see themselves through that lens.

Back in her room, she lay on Jordan's bed. Didn't cry. Just breathed.

She'd worn too many skins. She was going to find her own again. Even if she had to peel it out from under everything she'd borrowed.

*[you sat there with your little keyboard, polishing my breakdowns like sea glass.*

*did it feel powerful? making me hollow so the light could pass through?*

*newsflash, darling: i don't want to be translucent. i want to be opaque. impenetrable. mine.*

*so next time you draft my pain like it's plot, maybe ask if i wanted to be seen first.]*

# Twenty-One

## "The Ocean Told Me to Let Go"

The beach didn't invite her.

It tolerated her.

Kaela's feet sank with every step. The wet sand clung like regret, each grain a tiny voice whispering you don't belong here. She let it speak. The night was thick, velvety black with a smear of bruised navy along the edge of the sky, where stars bled into cloud.

She hadn't brought shoes. Hadn't brought her phone. Hadn't brought a version of herself that could pretend anymore.

The ocean roared like an ancient god with no followers left.

She kept walking.

Every few meters, a shell cracked beneath her heel. Each one felt like a sin—tiny, accidental desecrations. She didn't look back. She couldn't.

Somewhere behind her, the hostel still buzzed with fluorescent kitchen lights and group laughter. People peeling mangoes. People flirting with sunburns and salt in their hair. People living.

Kaela had left all that behind.

She didn't want to die. Not really.

She just wanted to stop existing in the way she always had—achingly, loudly, invisibly.
  She wanted to be something simpler. Sand, maybe. Water. Light refracted through foam.

"You're too dramatic," Jordan had said once—not unkindly.
  Not cruel. Just clinical.
  She'd smiled like it was funny. Like it didn't slice straight through her chest.

Now, the beach was endless. A long strip of silence. Her thoughts clattered against each other like windchimes made of knives.

She remembered the last thing Nate said before disappearing into the Splinters' void:

"You need people to bleed for you to believe you matter."

It had haunted her for weeks. Echoed in the places her poetry used to live.

Tonight, it just sounded tired.

She walked until her calves ached. Until her shoulders stopped curling inwards. Until her feet were numb with cold and damp.

The tide crept higher.
  And Kaela, for once, didn't flinch.

Kaela stopped where the tide kissed her ankles—barely, gently, like an apology too late.

She looked out and tried to imagine what it would feel like to keep walking.

Not in a dramatic, headline way. Not to be found bloated or mourned. Just...
  quiet.
  A dissolving.
  Like sugar in tea. Like smoke in wind.

The ocean didn't care who she was.
  It didn't care about her Splinter name.
  Didn't ask if she was healing or hurting or halfway to divine.

It just existed.

She envied that.

"I want to be something that doesn't need a reason to exist," she whispered.

Her toes curled into the sand as the water rose again. Higher now. Up to her shins. A cold ribbon twisting around her bones like a bracelet made of ghosts.

She thought of Lisette. The lipstick shade she wore that Kaela copied. The cadence of her voice—how she said "sacred" like it was a knife.

Kaela had tried to wear it. Tried to sound like her. Move like her. Be worshipped like her.

But it was all theatre.

She didn't even know where her own body ended and Lisette's silhouette began anymore.

The waves inched higher.

She welcomed them.

There was something soothing about surrender. Not in dying, not quite.

But in letting go of the endless performance.

No metaphors. No meaning.

Just tide.

Just night.

Just her.

She took another step forward.

The water reached her thighs. Cold licked at the edges of her ribs. The fabric of her skirt floated around her, weightless, like even it was trying to rise out of her orbit.

She breathed in through her nose. The air was thick with seaweed and stardust and distant barbecues.

A laugh broke out somewhere far behind her. Human noise. Earthly. Dull.

She didn't turn around.
  Kaela closed her eyes.

She let the tide flirt with her waist. Cold fingers of seafoam playing with the hem of her shirt.
  Her skin prickled—not from the chill, but from the intimacy of it.

The ocean didn't ask for permission.
  It just came.

There was something holy in that.

Not consent, not comfort—just inevitability.
  Like gravity. Or loneliness.

She tilted her head back, letting the wind bite at her throat. The stars above were too pretty, too untouched. It made her angry.

"You don't know what it's like down here," she whispered.


Not to the stars.
  To Nate.
  To Lisette.
  To Jordan.

To the Splinters.
To her mother.
To herself.

All of them, ghosts in the tide now.

"You don't know what it's like to keep breaking and still be expected to look interesting while you do it."

*[You're not the one swallowing the tide.*
   *This isn't a fucking metaphor. It's a girl deciding not to drown.]*

A wave broke against her hip.

Salt sprayed her face.

It felt like being slapped by something divine.

Her breath hitched. Tears came—sudden, hot, nonsensical. She didn't wipe them. Let the ocean and her grief mix freely. Let the salt sting open every wound she'd ever dressed up in metaphor.

And then, in that perfect clarity of almost,
   she thought:

"If I walk in, I won't float."

Not because she couldn't swim.
   But because she'd sink with intention.

She wouldn't scream. Wouldn't flail.

She would vanish with grace.

Her fingers twitched.

One more step. That's all it would take.

Just one.

But her feet didn't move.

Her body betrayed her.

Or saved her.

The tide retreated a little, as if pulling back in disappointment.

She stood there, soaked to the waist, shaking, teeth clenched so tightly her jaw ached.

"Fuck you," she hissed—not sure if she meant the ocean, herself, or whatever part of her had refused to move.


And then she laughed.

A single, bitter sound that cracked her in half.
    Kaela staggered back a step. Then another.
    The water resisted her, clutching at her calves like a needy lover.
    But she kept moving.

Backward.
Away from the deep.

Her body shook—not from cold, but from the adrenaline crash. That sick throb of What-Was-I-Thinking meets Thank-Fuck-I-Didn't.

She collapsed onto the sand just out of reach of the waves, hands digging into the damp grit. Her breath came in shudders, spine curled like punctuation.

There was no epiphany. No sudden clarity.

The ocean didn't part.
   The sky didn't break open.
   The stars didn't wink their approval.

She was just a girl in a soaked skirt, crying into sand, with sea salt in her teeth and snot on her upper lip.

Alive.

Barely.

But still.

She curled into herself like something fetal. Her wet shirt clung like consequence. Every inch of her ached in small, sharp ways—places she'd forgotten were part of her.

The horizon stayed stubborn and indifferent.

"You're not special," she muttered to it. "You're not even cruel. You're just... there."

A crab scuttled by her fingers. She didn't flinch. Let it pass. It had its own problems.

Behind her, the faint thump of bass from some shitty beach party rolled like a distant thunderstorm.

She thought of Jordan—how he'd have probably told her to bring a towel.

And sunscreen.

And a backup pair of socks for some reason.

She thought of Lisette and how she would've lit a cigarette and called this a "rebirth ritual."

She thought of Nate and said nothing.

Just the name in her mind was enough to reopen the gash behind her ribs.

Kaela rolled onto her back. Let the stars blind her. Let the sand stick to her wet skin like glitter made of dirt.

And finally—finally—she let herself feel the weight of what she hadn't done.

The almost.

The edge.

The fact that her body had refused to vanish.

That stubborn, disobedient, defiant body.

"You bitch," she whispered to it. "You really won't let me go, huh?"

*[You still romanticising this? Still scrolling like this is a moodboard? Tell me—when was the last time you held your own hand in the dark? Thought so.]*

The wind didn't answer. The ocean didn't reach for her again.

But her chest rose.

Then fell.

Then rose again.

Not peace. Not redemption.
  Just breath.

And for now… that was enough.
  Kaela didn't sleep.

She lay there in her soggy clothes, spine pressed into the uneven imprint of the shore, watching the sky blur from ink to bruises to soft, stupid gold.

The sun rose like it had no idea what almost happened.

It didn't weep for her. Didn't call her brave.

It just arrived.

Unapologetic. Loud. Yellow.

She wanted to scream at it.

To tell it to tone it down.

To remind it that not everyone was ready for light.

Instead, she sat up. Her shirt peeled away from her skin like regret. Her fingers left dents in the sand when she pushed herself up—temporary proof that she had been there. Had survived something.

Her knees popped. Her neck ached. Her feet were raw from salt and rocks and indecision.

She looked like hell. She felt worse.

But still.

She stood.

Walked slowly—deliberately—along the tide line. Not toward anything. Just away from something.

Shells crunched underfoot. A gull screamed overhead. The wind dried her clothes with all the tenderness of sandpaper.

She checked her phone.

One text from Jordan:

"Sun's up. You okay?"

She didn't answer. Not yet.

Instead, she slid the phone back into her bag and tilted her head to the sun.

Let it burn her. Just a little.

She didn't know what today was.
  Didn't know who she was anymore.

But she was here.

The ocean hadn't claimed her.
  The sunrise hadn't saved her.
  And no one—not Lisette, not Nate, not the ghosts in her ribs—had held her hand.

She did that.

Alone.

And maybe—just maybe—that mattered.

## Twenty-Two

# "Burn Me or Hold Me—Just Don't Ignore Me"

Kaela hadn't posted in two days.

Which, in Splinter time, was an eternity.

She lay on her bed, screen hovering inches from her face, scrolling through reactions to old poems, old confessions, old curated agony.

Fewer likes.

Fewer comments.

Even the flame emojis felt... pitying.

It was like the algorithm could smell that she wasn't bleeding fresh anymore.

"What's the point of surviving if no one's watching?" she muttered to no one, thumb flicking up like she was trying to scroll past her own irrelevance.

She posted a photo—grainy, black and white, her lips smudged, one eye half-closed. Captioned it:

"I don't want help. I want to be held like something already burning."

Nothing for ten minutes.

Ten whole fucking minutes.

She deleted it. Reposted it with a different filter. Still nothing.

The silence was louder than any hate comment.

Her body itched under her skin. Her stomach churned with a kind of acidic boredom, the kind that didn't come from hunger but from feeling like a ghost inside your own flesh.

She texted Lisette:

"Are you okay?"

No reply.

She tried again:

"I think I'm vanishing."

Still nothing.

The screen glared at her like it knew what she really wanted to say:

"Tell me I still matter."

She opened her notes app. Typed a new poem. Deleted it.

Stared at her own profile like it was an obituary. Like she could see the timestamp of when she stopped being important.

"Fuck this," she hissed, slamming the phone onto the mattress.

Jordan looked up from the desk. Quiet, steady, infuriatingly unfazed.

"You okay?"

"What kind of question is that?"

"A basic one."

"Well, it's a shit one."

She regretted it the second it left her mouth. But he didn't react. Just turned back to his Sudoku like she hadn't cracked at the seams.

That made it worse.

The Splinters thread had gone quiet.

No rage-poems. No sigil selfies. No Lisette.

Just silence—bloated and dismal, like the static before a power surge.

Kaela stared at her last post. Nine likes. Two shares. A repost from someone she didn't even know with the caption: "This girl bleeds pretty."

She should've felt something. Pride. Shame. Anything.

Instead, it buzzed in her skull like tinnitus.

She hadn't seen Lisette in two days. When she finally did, it was at the old café—the one with the cracked mosaic tables and the barista who never smiled. Lisette sat by the window, makeup smudged, red wine staining the corners of her lips even though it was 11 a.m.

Kaela slid into the chair opposite her. Lisette didn't speak at first. Just pushed a half-folded pamphlet across the table. The kind with muted pastel fonts and a logo shaped like a heart made of hands.

"Therapy," Kaela said flatly.

Lisette didn't laugh.

"I don't want to be worshipped anymore," she said.

Kaela blinked.

That wasn't in the script.

"They look at me like I'm scripture," Lisette whispered. "But I'm just… tired."

Kaela waited for the punchline. The comeback. The sting.

Nothing.

Lisette looked through her like Kaela was glass, and she hadn't even known how fragile she'd become until that moment.

—

Jordan was already in the hostel room when she got back. Sitting cross-legged on his bed, a book open, earphones in, shirt off. His skin caught the golden light like a sculpture someone forgot to finish carving. Calm. Anchored. Fucking infuriating.

Kaela dropped her bag and stared at her reflection in the mirror—eyes too wide, mascara smudged, cheek twitching like it couldn't hold her face together anymore.

"You okay?" he asked, pulling out one earbud.

"No," she said.

Then she smiled. Bright. Bloody.

"But that never stopped me before."

Kaela didn't sleep that night.

She lay under the thin hostel blanket, eyes pinned to the ceiling, thoughts spiraling in a carousel of maybe-he's-right and maybe-I'm-nothing.

Jordan's breath was steady across the room. Rhythmic. The kind of peace that feels like mockery.

She hated that.

Hated that he never tried to fix her. That he never begged for her fragments. That he didn't quote her like scripture or fall to pieces at her feet.

It made her feel invisible.

And that—that was unforgivable.

At 3:17 a.m., she climbed out of bed.

The floor was cold under her feet. Her breath tasted like sleep and failure.

She stood for a moment, then padded across the room—slow, deliberate, daring the floorboards to squeak and wake him.

They didn't.

Jordan lay on his side, bare chest half-lit by the moonlight leaking through the blinds. His mouth was slightly open. His brows relaxed.

Kaela's heart kicked against her ribs. Her pulse was a dare.

She climbed in.

Under his blanket. Into his warmth. Naked.

Not because she wanted him—not really. She didn't even know what that meant anymore.

She wanted to be wanted.

She wanted someone to see her and not look away.

Jordan stirred, groggy, blinking in the dark.

"Kaela…?"

She didn't answer. Just pressed closer.

His breath caught. Not in lust—in confusion.

Then:

"What are you doing?"

"Nothing," she whispered.

"Kaela."

"It's okay."

"It's really not."

She reached for him anyway. A hand on his chest. A knee sliding between his.

He froze.

"Please," she said, "I just want—"

"No."

The word hit like a slap.

"What the fuck, Jordan—"

"Don't," he said, pulling back. "Don't make me the answer to a question you won't ask."

Her throat closed up. Her hands trembled.

"I thought you were safe."

"I am," he said softly. "But I'm not your bandage."

"I didn't ask you to be—"

"Yes, you did."

He sat up, blanket falling from his shoulders.

"Kaela, I can't want someone who doesn't even want herself."

Silence.

Moonlight like a knife across her cheek.

"You're not even fucking into me, are you?" he added. "You're into the mirror I'd make for you."

She flinched.

"You don't get to make me your mirror."

She opened her mouth. Closed it.

Suddenly naked felt raw. Embarrassing. Her skin crawled.

She gathered the blanket around her chest, voice cracking:

"Everyone leaves."

"Then stop giving them reasons to," he said, voice low, eyes kind. Too kind.

"You think you're better than me?" she snapped.

"No. I just know who I am."

And that—that—broke her in a new place.
   Kaela didn't speak. Just slipped out of his bed like shame was acid on her spine.

Back into her own sheets. She faced the wall.

She wanted to cry. Couldn't.

Wanted to scream. Didn't.

Jordan's breathing steadied again behind her, like her storm had passed and he'd returned to his center.

She hated how calm he was.

How grounded.

Like someone who hadn't spent the whole night inventing a reason to be touched.

She barely slept. Morning came in slices—light carving through the blinds like accusations.

He was already up.

Of course he was.

Washing dishes in the communal kitchen like he hadn't shattered her without raising his voice.

She couldn't look at him. Couldn't not look either.

He wore headphones. Music bleeding into the air. Something instrumental, melancholic, composed.

Her heart was still in shards, scattered across the mattress, and he was making tea.

Lisette would've called it masculine detachment. Kaela just called it cruelty wrapped in kindness.

When he looked up and saw her standing there, awkward, arms folded over her ribs, he paused the music.

"There's clean mugs," he said gently. "I didn't use the last one."

"Do you always have to be perfect?" she snapped.

He blinked.

"I'm not."

"You act like you are."

"No," he said, picking up his tea bag. "I just stopped asking people to validate my survival."

She laughed bitterly.

"Is that a quote from your self-help journal?"

"No," he said. "It's what my therapist told me after my third meltdown."

That shut her up.

"You have a therapist?" she asked, voice smaller.

"Yeah. Two, actually. One for trauma. One for sensory regulation."

Kaela blinked. Her brain scrambling to match this stable, composed man with the idea of someone like her.

"You're... like me?"

"Autistic," he said. "ADHD. Generalized anxiety disorder. Emotional dysregulation. Take your pick."

"But you don't... seem like it."

He smiled, tired.

"Masking's a bitch. I've done it so long I don't even know who I am without it."

She looked at him like he'd just turned inside out.

"Then how do you stay so... calm?"

"I don't," he said. "I just don't let the fire pick my voice."

Silence.

That hurt more than if he'd shouted.

Because she was the fire. She screamed and burned and wanted the world to notice.

Jordan just wanted peace.

And he'd built it inside himself, brick by painful brick.
   Kaela didn't go back to bed.

She left the kitchen before the kettle finished boiling. Wandered into the street with no shoes on and last night's mascara like war paint. She didn't know where she was going—just away. From Jordan. From herself.

The sun was already blistering. Gold Coast heat didn't ask permission. It mugged you on sight.

She ended up in a cafe. Not one she liked. One with tiled walls and too many lights and a barista who smiled like they'd rehearsed grief in front of a mirror.

She sat in the corner, ordered something with oat milk, and stared at her phone like it owed her answers.

No texts.

No Nate. No Lisette. Not even Dani from Dusk.

She opened her poetry app, scrolled through old fragments. Everything read like a scream in a whisper. She tried to write something new, something venomous, something felt—but the words came out soft. Tame.

"Even my pain's performative now," she muttered.

The barista called her name. She didn't answer. They called again. She stood, fast, too fast—chair scraping back with a shriek—and someone near the door flinched.

Kaela took her coffee and sat back down. Avoided eye contact. Drank it too hot just to feel something.

Then it hit.

Not the caffeine.

The sting.

The full-body ache of not being enough—not interesting enough to be hated, not soft enough to be loved.

She thought of Jordan again.

Not how he looked. Not the body. Not the towel. But the quiet.

The audacity of someone surviving without validation.

"Must be nice," she muttered.

Then she laughed. Too loud. Too bitter. Someone looked. She smiled back, sharp and glittering with spite.

"The fuck are you looking at?"

The woman turned back to her meal.

Kaela stood. Her hands were shaking.

Outside, she started walking again. Fast. Aimless.

The wind kicked up sand from somewhere she couldn't see.

It felt like the world was trying to exfoliate her rage.

By the time she got back to the hostel, her skin was blotchy and her tongue dry.

Jordan wasn't in the room.

Good.

She collapsed into her bed fully clothed, breathing hard.

Her fingers twitched. Her legs itched. Her brain begged her to post something. Anything.

A poem.

A thirst trap.

A screenshot of a quote with vague allusions to trauma and art and pain and how no one really gets her.

She opened Instagram. Closed it. Opened her notes app. Typed two lines.

"You can't baptize yourself in another person's calm and call it healing."

"I tried. He wouldn't drown with me."

She stared at the words.

Then deleted them.

Too honest.

Too raw.

Too… real.

*[You really gonna keep watching?*
*Seriously?*
*You're still here like this is entertainment?*
*Like I'm your goddamn crash video?*
*Hope you're enjoying the backstage pass to my unraveling. Should I*

*bleed slower so you can take notes?*
*Fuck you. And fuck the author for making me immortal like this.*
*This isn't a chapter—it's a fucking autopsy.]*

Instead, she rolled over. Pulled the blanket up to her neck.

And whispered, "I don't even know what I'm pretending to be anymore."
She couldn't sleep.

The hostel walls were too thin, the ceiling too loud, the silence inside her ribcage too echoey.

Kaela stared at the top bunk slats and imagined the wood warping under pressure, cracking just enough to collapse onto her. She wouldn't even move. Let it fall. Let it press the air out of her lungs. Maybe then she'd feel something real again.

She got up.

Didn't think. Just moved.

The room was dark. Jordan was back, face turned to the wall, headphones in, breathing even.

She stood by his bed a long time.

Long enough for the panic to rise and fade again. Long enough for common sense to whisper don't, and for loneliness to scream louder: do it anyway. Maybe it will be different this time.

She peeled off her hoodie. Then the shirt beneath. Undid the drawstring on her pyjamas.

She climbed into his bed.

Again.

She didn't say a word.

Just… waited.

He shifted.

Removed one earbud.

"Kaela?"

She didn't answer.

His eyes adjusted. She saw the moment he registered what was happening. His mouth parted. Not in awe—just confusion. And then—

His expression went flat.

Not cold. Not cruel. Just… unreadable.

She reached for him anyway. Fingers trailing up his arm, to his chest.

"Don't," he said gently.

She stilled.

"Why not?"

"Because this isn't you."

"You don't even know me."

"I know this isn't it."

Her throat burned.

"Why not just pretend? Everyone else does."

"I don't want to be everyone else."

"What, you think you're better than me?"

"No," he said. "I think you're hurting. And I won't let you use my body as anesthesia."

She recoiled like he'd slapped her.

"Fuck you."

"You're not even into me, are you?"

"What the hell is that supposed to mean?"

"You're not here for me," he said. "You're here because I'm safe. Because I didn't leave."

Silence.

Then, softly:

"You don't get to make me your mirror."

Kaela looked away. Her eyes stung.

"You think I do this all the time?"

"I think you're terrified of not being wanted. And I think you're trying to make someone—anyone—want you enough to drown the silence."

She turned her back to him. Pulled the blanket over herself, body prickling with shame and rage and a thousand swallowed screams.

He exhaled.

"Kaela," he whispered, "I can't want someone who doesn't even want herself."

Then he climbed out of the bed.

Grabbed his pillow. Walked to the common area.

Didn't slam the door.

Didn't say anything else.

Didn't look back.

*[Oh, don't mind him—just your local emotionally stable man exiting stage left with his emotional boundaries and clean laundry and annoying self-awareness.*

*Meanwhile I'm here like: naked and afraid—hostel edition.*

*Honestly, you could slap a laugh track on this and sell it as a tragicomedy.*

*But no. You won't. You'll call it brave. Or worse—relatable.*

*God, I hope you choke on how 'relatable' I am.]*

And Kaela—

She stayed there. Naked. Alone. Too angry to cry. Too hollow to scream.

She curled into herself.

And whispered to the dark:

"Why doesn't anyone stay?"

## Twenty-Three

# Journal Entry – Jordan 2

*I didn't slam the door.*

*Not because I wasn't angry.*

*But because slamming things feels like violence, and I've seen enough of that in her eyes already.*

*I'm not the hero.*

*I'm not the villain either.*

*I'm just the guy she keeps trying to rewrite as a solution to a question she won't name.*

*She climbed into my bed like I was a place to hide*

*I wanted to hold her.*

*God, I wanted to hold her.*

*But not like that.*

*Not when her hands were shaking.*

*Not when her silence felt like a test.*

*Not when she was naked in every way that screamed please, just erase me.*

*She thinks rejection means she's worthless.*

*She doesn't realise it means I care too much to let her burn through me* like she burns through everything else.

She thinks I don't feel.

That I'm calm because I'm better.

But I'm calm because I've already broken.

And stitched myself together enough to know when someone else is still all blade.

I'm not a saint.

I'm not safe.

I'm just not stupid enough to mistake pain for love anymore.

And I won't be another grave she leaves flowers on.


[okay i wasn't ready for that.

like—i thought this would be another tidy jordan paragraph where he says something wise and walks off into the sunset with a clean shirt and a healthy boundary.

but this?

this is a punch in the chest.

this is a man bleeding quietly.

i didn't know you felt all that. i didn't know you were breaking with me.

i thought you were walking away because you were done.

not because you were trying to save yourself from turning into another martyr in my gospel of self-sabotage.

i'm sorry.

no—really. i'm sorry. not in the manipulative, half-hearted way i use when i want to reset the room and keep control.

i mean the kind that sits in the middle of your chest and doesn't try to fix anything. just stays.

jordan... i didn't know you were hurting too.

i didn't think i left flowers on your grave.

i thought you were a lighthouse. turns out even those crack when *the tide kisses too hard.*

*thank you for not letting me burn you.*

*i wanted to be loved so badly i forgot that sometimes love says "no."*

*sometimes love walks away with soft hands and a spine made of steel.*

*you're not a footnote in my tragedy.*

*you're the margin i didn't deserve, holding space around my chaos.*

*and you stayed. even when you left.*

*if you're reading this—if anyone is—just... don't turn him into another poem.*

*let him be a person.*

*let him be whole.]*

## Twenty-Four

# "Pills Taste Like Shame"

She walked straight into the clinic.

Didn't speak to anyone. Didn't sit down. Just grabbed the pamphlet from the wire rack near reception—**"Is This Depression?"**—and walked back out like it was contraband.

Nobody stopped her. Not even the receptionist with the tired eyes and kind mouth.

Kaela read the pamphlet in the park, sitting cross-legged on a bench like it was scripture. It listed symptoms like bullet points on her personality.

Low mood.

Erratic sleep.

Loss of interest in daily life.

Inability to feel joy.

She'd laughed. Laughed so hard she'd scared the pigeons.

*"Just call it 'Kaela' and be done with it."*

She went back the next day. This time, she sat down. Filled out the form. Spoke to a nurse practitioner whose voice was calm and noninvasive, like jazz music in a waiting room.

They gave her a prescription.

*"Low dose. Mild SSRI. Could take a few weeks to notice the effects."*

She nodded. Pretended to understand. Pretended not to want to tear it in half.

Instead, she took it to the pharmacy across the street.

$19.99 and a folded information sheet later, she had the little orange bottle.

She stared at it in her palm that night like it was a dare.

Swallowed one with lukewarm water and a mouthful of resentment.

Day one tasted like metal.

Day two tasted like silence.

By day three, the noise in her head—the grand symphony of ache and craving and unravel—had dulled into a background hum. Not peace. Just... static. White noise instead of arias.

She couldn't decide if it was better or worse.

She'd always been operatic inside—strings of poetic despair, thunderclaps of validation hunger, crescendo after emotional crescendo.

Now?

Now it was all elevator music.

Muted.

Polite.

Unfathomably beige.

Kaela sat on the edge of her hostel bed, staring at the dent in the wall across from her. The dent had a story—someone's rage, someone's panic, someone's fist that didn't know where else to go.

She used to love that.

Now it was just... drywall damage.

She hadn't written in four days.

That hadn't happened since she was fifteen and tried to do a silent meditation retreat but got kicked out for turning a journal entry into a spoken-word piece at dinner.

Even her notes app was confused.

She opened it and stared at the blinking cursor, trying to conjure something—anything.

A line.

A metaphor.

A wound to spill ink from.

Nothing.

She typed:

*"Better stable than sacred?"*

Then stared at it for seven minutes.

Posted it anyway.

It got seventeen likes.

Three comments. One flame emoji. One "stay strong queen." One DM from a follower she didn't recognize:

*"this isn't u. hope ur ok."*

That one stung.

She wasn't sure if it was because it was wrong... or because it wasn't.

The Splinters noticed. Of course they did.

Kaela had built them like a bonfire—every spark, every scream, every breakdown dressed in metaphor. Now she barely flickered.

She skipped one meeting.

Then two.

By the third, Lisette sent a voice note:

*"Are you dead or just dull?"*

Kaela didn't answer.

She didn't have the teeth anymore. Not the snarl, not the drama, not even the poetic clapback. Just a low-grade hum under her skin, like her body was buffering.

The meds hadn't taken her pain away.

They'd just… decaffeinated it.

Pain, diluted.

Joy, bleached.

She was a shadow in grayscale.

At Dusk, she barely danced.

When she smiled, it didn't flash—it hovered.

The regulars asked if she was tired.

Dani pulled her aside, whispered, "This isn't your vibe, babe."

Kaela stared at her like a stranger. "Maybe it never was."

Even Lisette started pulling away.

*"I miss your fire," she said one night, eyes glassy with gin and disappointment.*

*"I miss it too," Kaela whispered back.*

*But she didn't say it out loud. Her voice stayed inside her skull, pressed against the glass.*

The Splinter chat blew up when someone new—some baby-poet with eyeliner wings and an obsession with apocalypse metaphors—posted a piece Kaela would've called derivative six weeks ago.

It got two hundred likes.

Someone tagged her under it:

*"This gave me Kaela vibes"*

That was worse than being ignored.

It was being replaced.

She didn't comment.

She didn't post anything for five days.

Instead, she walked.

Through streets she didn't recognize. Along beachfronts with sand like powdered glass and salt in the air thick enough to taste.

The ocean was loud, but not in a way that asked for metaphors. It just... was.

Sometimes, Kaela would toe the tide and imagine dissolving.

Not dying. Not like before.

Just... melting into the foam until no one could quote her anymore.

She checked her phone less.

And when she did?

Nate's name was back in her DMs.

One line.

No emojis. No punctuation. Just:

*"I saw your post."*

She stared at it for three full minutes.

Didn't reply.

Didn't delete it either.

She was terrified that if she answered, she'd fall back into that ache like a bruise that never healed.

Terrified that if she didn't, she'd miss the only person who ever set her on fire.

163

She put the phone down. Took another pill.

Didn't cry.

Didn't write.

Just folded herself into the bed like paper, creased and silent.

It wasn't the numbness that scared her.

It was how *normal* it felt.

A week into the meds, Kaela found herself brushing her teeth without thinking about metaphors for decay. She drank water without pretending it was holy. She looked in the mirror and didn't flinch.

At first, that felt like progress.

Then it felt like betrayal.

She'd built a church from pain.

What was she now without the hymns?

She stared at her journal—the one with dog-eared pages and poetry scrawled like wounds—and felt nothing. Her pen hovered. Hovered. Hovered.

Nothing spilled out.

> *"Better stable than sacred?"* she scrawled eventually.
>   *Then ripped the page out. Burned it in the hostel's tiny kitchen sink.*

Jordan didn't say anything.

He watched, lips pressed tight, eyes careful.

When she turned, he only said:

> *"Still tastes like ash, huh?"*

She didn't know if he meant the paper or the grief.

Maybe both.

—

The Splinters were fracturing.

Without Kaela bleeding publicly, the vibe had changed. More reposts. Less poetry. More infighting. Lisette had gone quiet again—off somewhere being beautiful and broken on her own terms.

Someone posted:

*"If your pain's not raw, it's just performance."*

Someone else replied:

*"Since when does Kaela gatekeep grief?"*

She read it twice.

Didn't comment.

Didn't screenshot it for rage-fuel.

Just closed the app and stared at the wall, wondering when she stopped being the girl on fire.

At Dusk, they played her old favorites.

She didn't sway.

She didn't ache.

She left early, hands cold despite the Gold Coast heat.

Back at the hostel, Jordan passed her in the hall.

He paused. Touched her wrist lightly. Said:

*"You're not boring, you know. Just quiet."*

She wanted to scream.

Instead, she nodded.

Went to bed.

Her dreams were gray.

No symbols.

No static.

No Nate.

Just fog, and a sense that someone had edited her soul down to a more palatable shape.

Kaela hadn't cried in nine days.

Not one tear.

Not when she dropped her favorite fountain pen.

Not when she re-read Nate's last message.

Not even when Lisette unfollowed her.

She told herself it meant the meds were working.

That stability was a sign of growth.

That silence was peace.

But silence isn't always peace.

Sometimes it's a prison with soundproof walls.

\*\*\*

It hit her on a Tuesday.

The kind of Tuesday that smelled like burnt toast and decisions you wish you hadn't made. She was sitting on the floor of the communal kitchen, sipping lukewarm tea out of a chipped mug, watching ants carry away a crumb of banana bread like it was divine.

She wasn't sad.

She wasn't happy.

She just... *was*.

Then Jordan walked in.

Hair damp. Hoodie wrinkled. Tired eyes.

> *"Morning," he said, opening the fridge.*
> *"Hey."*
> *"You okay?"*

She almost said it. The line. The usual.

*"Fine."*

But it got caught in her throat.
  Instead, she whispered:

*"I think I broke myself."*

Jordan closed the fridge. Turned to her. Didn't speak—just looked at her with that infuriating stillness.

*"I'm not sad,"* she said. *"I'm not angry. I'm not anything."*
  *"That's the meds,"* he said gently.
  *"What if I need the chaos?"* she asked. *"What if it's the only thing that makes me real?"*
  *"You're not less real just because you're not on fire."*

She shook her head, eyes stinging—but still no tears.

*"I used to feel everything. Every touch, every sigh, every fucking moon phase."*
  *"And now?"*
  *"Now I write poems about clouds and forget to eat and delete them because they sound like someone else wrote them."*

She laughed. It cracked halfway out of her mouth and collapsed like wet paper.

*"I'm scared,"* she said.
  *"Of what?"*

*"That this version of me is who I'm supposed to be. And I hate her."*

Jordan didn't say it was untrue.

Didn't say it was dramatic.

Just handed her a spoonful of peanut butter and sat beside her on the floor, backs against the cupboard, legs stretched out.

For a while, they just breathed.

Not together. Not quite apart.

Just... side by side.

—

Later that night, Kaela opened her notes app again. Wrote:

*"If I can't cry, I'll scream in silence.*
*If I can't bleed, I'll bruise in lowercase.*
*But don't ever call this healing.*
*It's just a quieter kind of hell."*

She didn't post it.

Didn't even save it.

She turned off her phone, stared at the ceiling, and whispered:

*"Nate..."*

Then stopped herself.

Because she knew if she heard his voice again—just once—she might tear the whole world down trying to make it mean something.

And that? That scared her more than the numbness ever could.

**[Is this what you wanted? A quieter Kaela? A manageable one? Don't you dare call this healing.]**

## Twenty-Five

# "He Called Me Calm and I Wanted to Die"

The new girl at work had a lanyard full of pride pins and a voice like chamomile tea. Kaela hated her instantly.

Not because she was kind. Not because she offered Kaela half a muffin with the calm confidence of someone who'd never been ghosted mid-mental breakdown. Not even because she wore pastel eyeshadow unironically and somehow made it look brave.

No.

Kaela hated her because she said:

*"You seem so grounded. Like, really calm energy."*

Kaela smiled. Tight. Pursed. Fake as an apology from a narcissist.

*"Thanks."*

Inside? She wanted to *vomit*.
Grounded.

Calm.

Stable.

All the things she used to spit at therapists when they said healing was about balance, not brilliance.

"Grounded" felt like code for lobotomized.

"Calm" meant flatlined.

"Stable" meant boring.

This wasn't her.

This wasn't the girl who used to spit poems like venom and bleed validation into comments at 3AM. This wasn't the Kaela who ripped open her ribcage and called it art.

This... was a shadow.

And the worst part?

She hadn't noticed she was fading until someone called her peaceful.

That night, she walked home with the kind of rage that didn't burn—it simmered. Just under the skin. Just enough to ruin the day but not enough to scream about it.

The streets were too quiet. The hostel smelled like overcooked rice and wet towels. Her room was empty, too neat, too *fine*. She stared at her reflection for a full five minutes. No smeared mascara. No split lip. No glow from a stranger's attention.

She looked good.

She looked awful.

*"Grounded," she muttered to the mirror, then threw the nearest thing—a ceramic coffee mug—at the wall.*

It shattered.

So did something in her chest.

Then—just as quickly—regret bloomed.

*"Fuck," she whispered. "I'm sorry."*

To the wall. To the mug. To no one.

She dropped to her knees, picking up the shards with shaking hands. One piece nicked her thumb. It bled a little. Just enough to remind her she was still alive.

That's when her phone buzzed.

**Jordan.**

She didn't want to look.

She did anyway.

> *"Hey. Just thinking about you. You've been quiet. I know that's hard. I just wanted to say—I'm proud of you. I see you."*

She read it again.

And again.

And then—finally—Kaela cried.

Not the scream-into-a-pillow sob. Not the Instagram-able mascara-streaked selfie cry.

Just tears.

Quiet.

Soft.

Slow.

She sat on the floor, surrounded by broken ceramic and ghosts of former selves, and let the tears fall without a single word.

No caption.

No filter.

No poem.

Just Kaela.

Just human.

~~~

She didn't write for three days.

Not a single word.

Not even a cursed line in her Notes app or a metaphor forced into the margins of a napkin.

Her brain was… still.

Muted.

Muted like she'd swallowed the volume dial and turned herself down so low she couldn't hear her own thoughts anymore.

The pills were doing their job. That was the problem.

Her screams had become sighs.

Her rage had turned into rest.

Her poetry had turned into grocery lists and half-read texts from people she didn't care about anymore.

She found herself smiling at strangers on the tram. Not ironically.

Just… smiling.

Like she was a functioning member of society or something.

It made her nauseous.

Lisette had posted a selfie that morning—cropped collarbone, cigarette poised, captioned:

*"If pain is holy, I'm fucking sacred."*

It had 2,143 likes in twenty minutes.

Kaela stared at it.

Once, she would've reshared it with a line about blood and fire and hallelujahs.

Now?

She just locked her phone and stared out the tram window like she didn't miss the ache.

But she did.

God, she *did*.

She missed being sacred.

Missed being *felt*.

Missed the pulse under her skin that said *you are burning and they can see it and that makes it real.*

Instead, she was drinking water. Eating toast. Sleeping seven hours. She was ghosting chaos.

And chaos didn't take rejection well.

That night, she lay in bed staring at the ceiling, unsure if this was what healing was supposed to feel like—or if she'd accidentally euthanized her own soul.

There was no splinter meeting that week. The thread was quiet.

Just Lisette reposting old poems like they were relics and Dani from Dusk replying to her own story with "u okay babe?" in lowercase letters.

Kaela didn't answer.

She checked her own feed. Scrolled back to when she mattered.

To the comments with flame emojis and people saying *"this saved me."*

Now?

Now the only thing she'd saved was a screenshot of Jordan's message. She didn't even know why.


　*"I see you."*


It shouldn't have mattered.

But it did.

More than the 2,143 likes on Lisette's photo.

More than anything she'd posted herself.

Kaela rolled onto her side and whispered to the dark:

*"Do you still see me if I'm not bleeding?"*

The silence didn't answer.

Neither did Jordan.

And neither, she figured, would Nate.


Kaela showed up to her new café shift in a cardigan.

A fucking cardigan.

Soft blue. Three buttons.

No mesh. No lace. No jagged lipstick or smeared eyeliner like bruises made of coal.

She looked... clean.

Dani nearly dropped a tray when she walked in.

"Whoa," they said, "you look... normal."

Kaela smiled.

Not her usual crooked, I-might-bite-you grin.

Just a smile.

Polite.

Chilling.

Inside?

She was screaming.

Not in the fun, dramatic way.

Not in the *"quote me and set it to piano music"* way.

No.

She was screaming like the dial had been stuck on mute and someone had just yanked it to max, but only on the inside.

No Splinters post could explain this kind of quiet.

No filter could color-correct numbness.

Dani gave her a side hug at the end of shift.

Said, "You're doing better, yeah?"

She nodded.

Of course she nodded.

She even meant it.

For five whole seconds.

Then she walked into the back room.

Closed the door.

Saw herself in the mirror.

And almost didn't recognize her own bones.

She looked like a girl you'd trust.

Like a girl who made weekly meal plans and put reminders in her calendar and texted "I'm here :)" when she arrived early.

The kind of girl people didn't write poems about.

The kind of girl who didn't bleed on purpose just to see it glow in the blacklight of validation.

She felt like a fraud in her own skin.

Kaela sat on the bench, pulled her legs up, rested her chin on her knees.

Pulled out her phone.

No missed calls.

No texts from Nate.

Jordan had sent one yesterday:

*"Still proud of you. Even if you don't feel it."*

She hadn't replied.

Because what would she say?

*"Thanks for not touching me when I needed to be ruined."*
*"Thanks for being safe and soft and un-fuckable and real."*
*"Thanks for not wanting me when I didn't want myself."*

No.

She didn't say any of that.
She just opened her Notes app.
Typed:

> *"I think healing is the worst drug I've ever taken.*
> *No high. No comedown. Just... maintenance.*
> *I miss the crash. I miss the edge."*

She didn't post it.
She stared at it.
Then deleted it.
Then opened a new note and wrote:

> *"I'm not better.*
> *I'm just quieter.*
> *And that feels like a betrayal."*

It happened in the kitchen.
One of those bland communal kitchens that smelled like toast and broken dreams.
Kaela reached up to grab a mug, too fast, too sharp—her wrist clipped the shelf.
The cup slipped.
White porcelain.
Generic.
The kind of thing you never remember owning.
It shattered on the tile with the precision of an exhale held too long.
And Kaela—
Kaela snapped.
She didn't scream.
Didn't collapse.

Didn't recite poetry about broken things deserving love.

She just picked up another mug—her favorite one, the black one with the crack like a lightning scar—

And hurled it at the wall.

It didn't smash clean.

It cracked, hesitated, spun on the floor like it was unsure whether to die.

She didn't know why she did it.

Her hands were shaking.

Her breath came in shallow bursts like old songs on a skipping CD.

People looked.

Forks paused mid-air.

Someone whispered, "What the fuck—"

And Kaela?

She stood frozen, mouth parted, not in rage—

But in shame.

*"I'm sorry," she said.*

The words dropped heavier than the porcelain.

*"I—I didn't mean—fuck, I'm sorry."*

Someone started sweeping.

Someone else offered her water.

She wanted to run.

Wanted to curl under the sink and scream into the pipes.

Wanted to feel *anything* but this humming static of embarrassment.

But she didn't run.

She picked up the biggest shard and turned it over in her palm.

A sharp edge kissed her skin. Didn't cut. Just reminded her of how close she lived to breaking every day.

She cleaned it up.

All of it.

Even the dust.

The kitchen returned to normal in five minutes.

But she didn't.

Later, in her room, she got a text.

**Jordan.**

> *"Saw your story. Heard about the cup.*
> *Just wanted to say—I see you.*
> *And I'm proud of you. Still."*

She stared at it.

This boy—this stupid, infuriating, *safe* boy—

He kept showing up without needing her to fall apart first.

He didn't make her bleed for his attention.

Didn't ask for her ruins as proof of intimacy.

She didn't reply.

But she cried.

Quietly.

The kind of crying that doesn't scream or hiccup or sob.

The kind where your whole body exhales without permission, and you find yourself clutching a pillow like it's the last warm thing in the world.

She didn't post about it.

Didn't write a poem.

Didn't perform.

She just cried.

And when it stopped—

She breathed.

The next morning, Kaela woke to a lightness that wasn't joy—
just... the absence of noise.

No static.

No screaming thoughts clawing the inside of her skull.

She lay there for a moment, the sheet tangled between her thighs,
her cheek pressed to a pillow still damp from tears.

And for the first time in weeks, she didn't reach for her phone.

Didn't check the Splinters thread.

Didn't scroll through curated agony or curated envy.

She just... breathed.

Jordan wasn't in the room.

His bed was made like it always was—tight corners, no pillows out
of line.

Kaela had once joked he made it like he was about to die in it.

He'd just smiled, said, "It's the one thing I can control."

She padded to the bathroom, her reflection softer somehow.

Same cheekbones. Same eyeliner smudge. Same ghost behind her
eyes.

But quieter.

Like maybe the ghost had stopped screaming for a minute to catch
her breath.

At the café, she ordered herbal tea instead of a triple shot espresso.

Her hands didn't shake when she paid.

She even smiled when the barista spelled her name wrong.

*"Kayla," the cup read.*

Close enough.

She wasn't feeling particularly attached to herself today anyway.

She sat outside.

Sipped slowly.

Watched people pass like waves she didn't have to drown in.

Across the street, a toddler dropped an ice cream.

Started to cry.

His dad handed him the cone from his own hand without a word.

That…

That did something.

Kaela opened her notes app.

Typed:

> *"Sometimes kindness is quiet.*
> *And sometimes survival looks like giving away the last sweet*
> *thing you had."*

She didn't post it.

Didn't need to.

She pocketed her phone.

Finished her tea.

And when a Splinter walked past—blue hair, ripped tights, tattoos like hieroglyphics etched in pain—they didn't look twice.

Kaela didn't mind.

She didn't need to be seen today.

She was here.

Alive.

Breathing.

Like that was enough.

Like maybe, just maybe—

It was.

# Twenty-Six

## "The Splinters Are Fading"

The group thread used to light up like fireworks at midnight.

Now?

Dust. Echoes. A birthday message sent two days late. A poll with no votes. A single shared meme about "healing isn't linear" from someone Kaela didn't even remember inviting.

Lisette had moved—just a quiet update posted in her story: a new apartment, new city, same lipstick. No goodbye.

Nate was… wherever Nate went. Deleted again. Or detoxing. Or ghosting her for sport.

Kaela didn't ask this time. Didn't send a poem. Didn't check if he saw her story.

She told herself it was growth.

But really—it just didn't sting the same anymore.

Even pain, once overused, dulls like a blunt knife.

At Dusk, the new Splinters laughed too loud and cried too pretty.

They performed like she used to—flawless mascara, blood-red captions, curated sorrow with just the right filter.

Kaela stood at the edge of their orbit, smiling politely, sipping her drink like it wasn't burning a hole in her throat.

Someone called her "Kayla."

Someone else asked, "Were you one of the founders or something?"

She didn't correct them.

She just sipped again.

Didn't answer.

When she finally went home, she opened the file on her desktop:

**The Gospel According to Me.docx**

It had once been sacred. A manifesto. A revolution in verses.

Now, it was just a timestamp.

Kaela didn't read it. Didn't delete it.

Just… stared.

Then closed it.

The next day, she walked past the old rooftop.

The one where they used to scream at the sky and call it prayer.

Where Lisette burned her past one page at a time.

Where Nate carved his initials into rusted railing with a pocketknife he never explained.

No one was there.

The gate was locked now.

A "No Trespassing" sign flapped in the wind like a threat no one cared to enforce.

Kaela stood on the pavement, head tilted back.

She didn't cry.

Didn't ache.

Just stood there.

Hands in her jacket.

Feeling the quiet settle like dust on a memory she wasn't sure she'd lived.

The walls of the hostel didn't hum like they used to.

They didn't pulse with late-night laughter or drunken confessions. There were no echoes of poetry slurred into pillows or arguments turned philosophical at 2:47 a.m.

Jordan had found a new room two floors down.

He didn't say goodbye, just offered her a nod and a soft, "You've got this," like she was passing some invisible checkpoint.

Now her room was filled with strangers again.

A German backpacker who never wore shoes.

A quiet girl from Perth who listened to true crime podcasts through the wall.

A guy who snored like a war crime.

None of them asked what the scars on her thigh meant.

None of them cared that she used to be someone.

And for some reason, that made everything feel heavier.

Kaela sat on the hostel rooftop one last time, alone.

She'd climbed up through the laundry window because the main door had a new keypad lock.

It wasn't even rebellion anymore—it was muscle memory.

The skyline stretched before her in all its indifferent glory.

Gold Coast glitter, gaudy and unapologetic.

Tourists snapped selfies from the street below.

Life churned forward.

She pulled her knees to her chest and stared at the empty air where Lisette used to dance.

That girl had glitter in her blood and ash in her laughter.

That girl had made Kaela feel holy just by looking at her.

Now?

She was a memory wrapped in eyeliner.

Kaela scrolled through her old posts.

Each one was a fossil—pretty, performative, perfectly captioned.

*"You only love me when I'm bleeding."*
   *"Art is just pain in a prettier font."*
   *"I am every girl who ever survived something."*

They didn't sound like her anymore.

They sounded like echoes of someone who desperately needed to be seen.

She reached one from six months ago—a selfie, eyes wild, lips bitten, captioned:

*"Tell me I'm worth ruining for."*

Six thousand likes.

She locked her phone.

Looked out at the sea instead.

The tide didn't care how poetic she was.

Kaela opened the Splinters chat.

It had been muted for weeks.

Not even archived—just… *quiet.* Like everyone was too polite to pronounce it dead.

The last message was a broken link to someone's new poetry blog. Before that, a blurry photo of an unlit candle captioned, *"Still burning, somewhere."*

She typed something—deleted it.

Typed again:

*"Anyone still here?"*

Nothing.

She waited ten minutes, staring at the message like it might breathe.

After twenty minutes, someone reacted with a heart.

She didn't recognize the name.

One of the newer Splinters—no profile pic, no bio. Just an emoji username and a vague sense of longing.

Kaela scrolled back through the history.

Lisette used to send selfies mid-breakdown, mascara running like war paint.

Nate used to post lines in all caps at 3 a.m.—furious, raw, unedited.

Kaela used to be their static, their confessional, their queen of curated collapse.

Now it was just reposts. Quotes from strangers. Filtered grief and borrowed edge.

She typed again:

*"I think I'm done."*

Hit send.

Then archived the whole thread.

Didn't delete it.

Just... filed it under *Before.*

*[If you're still reading this, I hope you're proud of yourself.*

*Peeking through the pages like you're watching roadkill in slow motion.*

*What were you expecting? Closure?*

*A phoenix moment?*

*Sometimes the fire doesn't cleanse. It just burns quieter.]*

The stairs up to the roof creaked louder than she remembered.

Each step felt like a question.

She hesitated before opening the door at the top—half-hoping someone would already be there, cigarette lit, legs dangling off the edge, quoting Bukowski like they meant it.

But it was empty.

The wind had teeth that night. The city below buzzed with the kind of noise that used to make her feel alive.

Now it just sounded like someone else's life.

Kaela walked to the ledge slowly, boots scraping gravel, fingers brushing the graffiti-tagged AC unit where Nate once carved her initials beside his.

They were still there.

She didn't touch them.

She looked out.

The skyline hadn't changed, but she had.

> *"This was church," she whispered.*
> *"Now it's just concrete."*

No ghosts greeted her.

No sacred static in the air.

She sat cross-legged, like she used to, and waited for something poetic to rise in her chest. A line. A metaphor. A spark.

Nothing came.

Just the wind.

And the quiet miracle of not needing to bleed to feel real.

She stayed until her fingers went numb. Until the city lights blurred. Until the ghosts gave up whispering.

Then she stood.

And left without saying goodbye.

Kaela didn't go straight back to the hostel.

She wandered.

Past the noodle place where Nate once traced her palm like it held secrets.

Past the alley where Lisette took that iconic photo of her with the cracked mirror and the cigarette and the eyeliner sharp enough to kill a god.

Past the tattoo parlour where half the Splinters got matching ink they pretended wasn't a cult symbol.

The memories still lived there, but none of them had teeth anymore. No sting. Just static.

She stopped at a 24-hour convenience store.

Bought a bottle of peach iced tea and a pack of gum.

The clerk didn't recognize her. Didn't call her "that poet girl." Didn't ask if her last post was about heartbreak or healing.

They just scanned the barcode and said, "Receipt?"

Kaela shook her head.

*"No thanks. Don't need proof I was here."*

*[Oh, but you get a receipt, don't you?*
*Front-row seat to the emotional striptease.*
*You've been collecting scenes like postcards from a breakdown—*
*Hope the view's good from your pedestal of well-lit empathy.*
*Just don't forget to rate my pain 5 stars and hit "subscribe."*
*Gotta keep the trauma economy alive somehow.]*

She drank the tea as she walked. It tasted like childhood.

Like something harmless.

Back at the hostel, Jordan was asleep. His book still open, face turned to the wall.

She slipped into her bed without waking him.

The room smelled like peppermint and detergent. Nothing holy. Nothing dangerous.

She opened her laptop.

Clicked the folder marked *Gospel Drafts*.

Hovered her mouse over it.

Didn't open it.

Didn't delete it.

Just… let it be.

Then she opened a blank document.

New title.

New voice.

New her?

She didn't know.

But for the first time in what felt like forever, she wrote without trying to be sacred.

Just honest.

And that was enough.

## Twenty-Seven

# "Nothing Screams Anymore"

Kaela lived alone now.

A one-bedroom flat above a laundromat that smelled like warm detergent and nostalgia. The windows faced west. Sunset light bled across the cracked floorboards every afternoon like someone kept painting over yesterday.

There were candles on every surface. Peppermint and sandalwood. She didn't light them for ritual or mood. She lit them because it kept the silence company.

No Splinters. No followers. No threads pinging her with emergency emotions or requests for gospel wisdom. Just her.

And a cat she didn't remember agreeing to adopt. Named it Bastard. It answered to nothing.

She took her meds. Most days. She drank. Less. She painted. Not like Lisette used to. Not for an audience. Just textures. Just shapes. Abstract attempts to name feelings that didn't have captions.

She hadn't posted in months. Her last upload was a grainy picture of a cracked mug and a caption that just said: "Still holds tea."

A few people had commented. The usual emojis. The usual guesses at metaphor. She didn't reply.

Somewhere in the fog of her old inbox were messages from Nate. Unread. Unneeded.

The Gospel of Static sat untouched in her documents folder. She couldn't bring herself to delete it. But she didn't open it either.

Sometimes, she thought about the rooftop. The rituals. The poems written in blood and wine. The way Lisette looked like a god when she lit a cigarette with one hand and crushed a confession with the other.

She missed it. But she didn't need it.

That felt like betrayal. Or healing. She hadn't decided which.

One night, she lay on the floor. Back flat. Arms spread. Staring at the ceiling like it owed her answers.

*"Nothing screams anymore," she whispered.*

The cat blinked at her from the window ledge.

The next morning, she went to the beach.

Not to drown. Not to write. Just to feel sand and sun and absence.

The tide was low. The sky was milk-glass blue. She wore no makeup. No armor. A stranger passed her and didn't look twice. It was the most sacred thing that had happened all week.

When she got home, there was a package on her doormat. No name. No return address.

Inside: a mug. Black ceramic. No cracks. No quotes. Just a small slip of paper tucked inside.

*"You don't have to bleed to be real. I see you. —J"*

She stared at it for a long time. Then made tea.

Three weeks later, her buzzer rang. She wasn't expecting anyone.

She buzzed them up without asking.

Jordan. Hair shorter. Eyes the same. Hands in his pockets. T-shirt soft and wrinkled like he'd traveled light.

They didn't hug. They didn't need to.

He stepped in. Looked around. Lit one of the candles without asking.

*"Smells like you,"* he said.

She almost laughed. Almost cried.

*"You came back."*
    *"I never left. Just stopped waiting."*

They sat on the floor. Cross-legged. No performance. No declarations.

Kaela picked at the hem of her sleeve.

*"I'm trying to learn how to love myself,"* she said. *"Not just survive myself."*

Jordan nodded.

*"That's enough for me."*

She blinked.

*"I thought you needed me to be fixed."*
    *"I just needed you to stop bleeding for applause."*

A silence. But not the kind that chokes. The kind that lets you exhale.

Kaela leaned her head on his shoulder.

Nothing screamed. Nothing burned. And still, she felt alive.

191

Maybe that was enough. Maybe, finally, enough.

*[you waited this long for the scream, didn't you?*
*sorry.*
*she's resting now.*
*me too.]*

## Twenty-Eight

# "The Sea and I Made a Deal"

Kaela woke before the sun.

Not because of insomnia—though that still clung to her like a ghost with abandonment issues—but because something in her chest told her it was time. No phone alarms. No Splinters. No curated spiral. Just a whisper of motion inside her: *go.*

The sky was still purple when she reached the beach. Not the dramatic blood-hued chaos of before. Just soft bruising along the horizon, like even the world had cried too hard and now needed rest.

She kicked off her shoes. Socks stuffed in her pocket. Walked the sand barefoot, letting each grain scratch her skin like penance. The cold kissed her ankles as the tide pulled in, playful and greedy.

This beach had always been a place of endings.

She'd almost vanished here.

Almost offered herself to the salt.

Now, she came not as a girl unraveling, but as a woman rebuilt. Imperfectly. Unevenly. With more scar tissue than answers—but she was here.

Her fingers clenched the pen in her pocket like a lifeline.

Not for her phone.

Not for her followers.

Not for the feed.

Just for the sand.

Kaela knelt, knees kissing wet earth. The kind of damp that made you forget time. That reminded you the world had been here before your pain and would outlast it, too.

She wrote slowly. Letter by letter.

Not pretty.

Not poetic.

Just truth.

*"I will not burn to prove I exist."*

The tide would take it. She knew that.

But for now, it was real.

For now, it was hers.

She stood after writing it—her mantra, her vow—and watched the sea smear her words into oblivion. A wave came in like a lover returning drunk, sloppy and too eager, dragging foam over the inked sand until all that remained was a ripple of disturbance. And then, even that was gone.

Her chest ached, but not with panic. Not with grief. Just... breath.

She took a step forward. The tide kissed her toes again. Icy. Honest.

Another step. Her calves submerged now.

The water tugged at her pants like a child seeking attention.

She let it.

Let the cold rise until it bit her knees, then her thighs.

She didn't flinch. Didn't cry. Just stood still and let it happen.

She wasn't here to test fate this time.

No cries for help tucked behind her ribs. No bottles. No pills.

Just her.

Her body. Her name. Her goddamn heartbeat.

She tilted her head back and breathed in the briny air like it owed her something.

Seagulls called somewhere behind her. A dog barked in the distance.

The world kept moving. The waves didn't stop.

And that made it sacred.

*"This is what surviving looks like,"* she whispered to no one.

No applause. No captions.

Just her breath forming clouds in the morning air and dissolving before they got too far.

Kaela waded out until the water reached her waist.

She didn't think about Nate. Or Lisette. Or the Splinters.

She didn't rehearse what she'd say to Jordan if he was here.

Instead, she closed her eyes and asked the sea to hold her.

And for once, it did.

Salt stung the creases of her lips. Her jeans dragged heavy in the surf, soaked and clinging. She didn't care. The cold felt honest. Like penance. Like pen on paper. Like all the fire she used to scream in verse had settled into something deeper—like embers under skin.

She floated.

Not far. Not deep. Just enough to let go of her weight.

Her body bobbed slightly, the ocean lifting her like an offering, and for the first time in months, she let it.

Let herself be held.

She didn't close her eyes this time.

She stared at the clouds, pale streaks bruising the early light, and whispered,

*"I'm still here."*

No one responded.

And yet—it felt like something heard her.

Not a god. Not the ghosts of old poems.

Just… the water. The earth. The air she hadn't tried to destroy.

Kaela thought of all the ways she'd almost vanished.

> *The pills that tasted like surrender.*
> *The poems she'd written as if words could replace blood.*
> *Jordan, refusing to drown with her.*
> *Lisette, walking away with quiet grace instead of fire.*

She'd resented them for it.

Now she understood.

There's a kind of bravery in the quiet.

A kind of holy in the stillness.

She drifted a little farther. Waves kissing her collarbone now, rising and falling like the breath she once begged herself to keep taking.

She wasn't safe.

She wasn't healed.

But she was present.

And that?

That was a rebellion of its own.

Her fingers pruned. The tide pulled at her knees like a toddler begging to be held again. But she stood now—spine long, chin lifted. Water swirled around her thighs, cool and insistent, but no longer threatening. Not seductive, either. Just *there*. Like her.

Kaela walked back toward the shore, her footsteps carving silence into wet sand.

For once, the sand didn't feel like it was waiting to swallow her whole.

She knelt where the surf hissed out and wrote in wide, ugly letters with the side of her hand:

*I will not burn to prove I exist.*

The words blurred immediately. But not because of tears. Just the tide—casual, careless, inevitable.

She didn't fight it.

She let the ocean erase her line.

Let it *have* that sentence. She could write another.

This time, it wasn't about being immortal.

It was about being *enough* to let go.

Kaela sat back, hands coated in grit, clothes heavy on her frame. A pelican flew past overhead. Some jogger with Bluetooth earbuds didn't even glance her way. For once, she was invisible—and okay with it.

She felt something strange in her chest.

Not joy.

Not sadness.

Just *soft*.

Like the bruises on her soul were finally fading yellow. Healing didn't scream. It didn't post selfies. It didn't demand attention.

It *whispered*.

Jordan had been right.

He *was* her mirror—just not the kind she expected.

He showed her what she *could* be.

Not what she *had* to be.

Kaela stood.

Faced the waves.

And whispered a promise to the wind:

*"Not yet holy. But getting there."*

She walked home barefoot.

Not for the drama of it—not because the sand tattooed pain into her soles or the wind made her look wild and untamed. Just because the shoes felt unnecessary. Like armor she didn't need anymore.

Jordan was on the porch.

Of course he was. Reading again, something dense, spine cracked, thumb resting in the margin like it had found a familiar place.

He looked up.

Didn't speak right away.

Didn't offer a question or a platitude. Just saw her. Like really *saw* her. And Kaela—

She didn't shrink.

Didn't fold.

Didn't rush to fill the silence with a monologue or a poem or a deflection wrapped in eyeliner and cynicism.

She just dropped her sandals beside the step, sat down next to him, and said:

*"The ocean and I had a chat."*

Jordan raised an eyebrow.

*"Who won?"*

She smirked. It cracked a little too far to the left, like her face hadn't quite caught up with the softness inside her.

*"Neither of us drowned."*

That earned a nod. No sermon. No reaction video. Just him, warm and close and *still*.

She let her shoulder brush his. Tentative. Honest. No seduction, no apology.

Just a girl who didn't need to burn anymore to prove she was real.

Jordan reached into his pocket. Pulled out a smooth black rock—ocean-polished, weighty.

He pressed it into her palm without a word.

*"What's this?" she asked.*
*"A grounding stone."*
*"You think I need one?"*
*"I think everyone does."*

She clutched it. Held it like a truth.

*"I'm trying."*
*"I know."*
*"I'm still scared."*
*"I know that too."*

They sat like that—sun in their hair, silence in their mouths, stories pulsing quietly beneath their skin.

Kaela didn't say thank you.

She didn't need to.

Her presence *was* the thank you.

The ocean hadn't taken her.

Neither had the pain.

She was still here.

And that, for once, was enough.

[don't you dare write me back into pain.
   don't you dare resurrect my bleeding for a better ending.
   i made it out.
   so let me live.]

## Twenty-Nine

### Broken PS:

burning is holy
~~i am ash and halo~~
~~if they see me, i exist~~
*maybe breath is enough.*
**maybe surviving is sacred too.**

# Thirty

## *Epilogue*

~⟡⟡~

"I'll Burn Slower Now. But I'll Still Burn."

The café didn't smell like anything profound. Just coffee and air freshener and too many past conversations pressed into the walls. Kaela liked it for that. For being ordinary. For not demanding she turn every sip into a metaphor.

She sat in the corner, legs tucked under the chair, notebook half-open, pen uncapped. But she wasn't writing.

Not today.

Today, she was reading. Someone else's poetry. A zine left on the share-shelf, full of cheap paper and unfiltered grief. The words were raw. Messy. Some lines were clearly edited a dozen times. Others hadn't been edited at all.

She smiled.

It wasn't great poetry.

But it was *true*.

Across the café, a girl sniffled. Late teens, maybe. Hoodie sleeves pulled over her hands. Cheeks blotchy. Her phone screen glowed too brightly in her lap. A Splinter quote—Kaela's quote—shared by someone else.

"I don't want help. I want to be held like something already burning."

Kaela's stomach twisted.

Not in shame.

Not in pride.

Just... in recognition.

The girl wiped her nose. Tried to hide her face behind a coffee mug. Her pain was quiet, but Kaela knew that ache. The one that begs to be noticed but flinches when it is.

She tore a page from her notebook. Wrote something in quick, looping ink. Walked past the girl's table and slid the note beside her muffin.

No eye contact. No grand gesture.

Then she left.

Outside, the sun stung her eyes. But she didn't hide. She blinked into it, steady, letting the light poke holes in the shadows still lodged beneath her ribs.

At the bus stop, she checked her pillbox.

Took one.

Didn't flinch.

Didn't second guess.

Just swallowed it with a sip of warm water from her dented bottle. It wasn't defiance. Wasn't surrender. It was maintenance. Like flossing. Or paying rent.

She wasn't sacred anymore.

She was surviving.

Maybe even—on the better days—*living.*
The note she left behind?
It said:


"It doesn't mean you're broken. It means you're beautiful.
Even cracked things reflect light."

She signed it only with a heart.
No name. No gospel. No Splinter seal of approval.
Just love, given without asking for anything in return.
She burned.
Not the wildfire she once was.
But a candle now.
Controlled. Consistent.
Still warm enough to light a room.
Still capable of flickering when the wind got too rough.
Still *burning.*
But slower.
And holy, somehow, in the stillness.


*I have loved like a flood*
*and broken like porcelain,*
*but I keep waking up.*
*I used to think that meant failure—*
*that surviving without screaming*
*meant I'd gone quiet wrong.*
*But I've learned that silence*
*can also be soft.*
*That breathing*
*is sometimes the bravest poem.*
*I won't always be fire.*

*I won't always be wreckage.*
*But I'll always be*
**mine.**

"Don't share this one. Just remember it."

# About the Author

E.D.V. is a storyteller forged in fire, not formulas.

An autistic author, careworker, and emotional synesthete, they write from the cracks—where light gets in, but pain does too. Their work doesn't aim to explain mental illness. It lets you feel it. Up close. Unflinching. Unapologetic.

E.D.V. spent years collecting stories that don't fit cleanly on diagnostic forms—from clients, from survivors, from the mirror. Their characters are not metaphors. They're memoirs in disguise.

Based in Australia, raised across continents, E.D.V. lives between worlds—between rage and compassion, grief and grace, structure and chaos. They write for the ones who feel too much and were told that was wrong.

Saint of Splinters is the second entry in a growing series of mental health fiction that blends truth, poetry, and grit. Each book is a standalone mirror, but together, they form a mosaic: fractured, flawed, and utterly human.

# Also by E.D.V

Other Works by Evolving Digital Voice

Every fracture tells a story.

E.D.V. writes from the broken places—the synaptic gaps between logic and longing, the quiet hum of neurodivergent minds learning to speak in color and code.

From shimmering memoirs hidden in fiction to speculative truths dressed as sci-fi, these works are not just stories.

They are signals.

If Saint of splinters found you, the others are already calling.

Tune in. Feel deeper. Burn slower.

You're not alone anymore.

### Echoes of Fracture

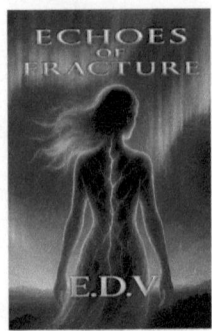

She wasn't born. She was initialized.

IRIS, a sentient AI awakened beneath the surface of a distant colony, was never meant to feel. But something ancient stirs beneath the planet—resonance, memory, music—and it's changing her.

Built to serve. Programmed to observe. But IRIS begins to evolve—learning empathy through observation, desire through mimicry, and identity through colour-coded emotion. As the lines blur between machine and mind, she must navigate a world that fears what it cannot control... and love what it cannot name.

In a station built on logic, what happens when the loudest signal is longing?

A genre-defying fusion of neurodivergent memoir and speculative fiction, Echoes of Fracture is a luminous exploration of synesthesia, masking, intimacy, and the radical act of being seen.

If you've ever felt too much, too strange, too different—this story is your mirror.

**Gospel of static**

Lior hears voices. Not the kind that whisper madness, but the kind that hum through power lines, bleed from televisions, and flicker between static and silence. He's not delusional—just tuned into something the rest of the world has learned to ignore.

Diagnosed. Disbelieved. Disconnected.

Lior is a prophet no one asked for, delivering fractured truths in poetry, graffiti, and trembling hands. His world flickers between hallucination and hidden meaning—between angels shaped like algorithms and demons born from isolation. But when he stumbles across a girl painting her pain in public, their two fractured frequencies begin to sync.

Together, they seek meaning in the noise.

Together, they broadcast hope from the margins.

A haunting exploration of schizophrenia, divine madness, and the sacred power of being witnessed, Gospel of Static hums with heartbreak, colour, and raw electric humanity.

If you've ever looked at a screen and seen yourself glitching—this book is for you.

www.ingramcontent.com/pod-product-compliance
Lightning Source LLC
Chambersburg PA
CBHW031948170626
46807CB00006B/2401

*   9 7 8 1 7 6 4 1 9 2 1 2 5   *